Finding Nowhere

Jeff Wade

Prologue

"The past is dead and gone," he said. "You made amends for what you done. Ain't no sense digging up old bones now."

Still she sighed, and prattled on with her apologies, but placidly now as he calmed her. His leather hands were an ogre's hands, each cigar finger capped with nails like hammered coins; but his hands were also lover's hands, tender as he toyed with her silky blond ponytail.

Somewhere deep in the woods, a whippoorwill crooned a serenade. Moved by the tune, an owl asked its one-word question, expecting no reply. A chorus of frogs seemed indifferent to the dirge.

Outside the trailer, long-dead junkers posed on blocks, prehistoric carcasses frozen mid-step. A shovel seemed to prop up the corpse of a tree. Arisen from a sea of weeds, vines like tentacles choked a sapling, dragging it down into the depths.

Inside, a glass-eyed deer kept vigil from the wall, forlorn, as if wondering, *where's the rest of me?* The TV slept with one eye open. The floor was lined with threadbare carpet, the air thick with the stink of stale coffee and a hint of decay.

A dim light glowed from the back room, where his caresses continued. "Shhhh . . . You hush now. I don't care who you was back then. I love you just the way you are, *right now.*"

He shook his head and sighed, then draped her over the coffee table. Smoothed her over the surface. He fingered the hair . . . searching . . .

When he located the eyelet, he lifted the ponytail to a hook depending from the ceiling. Careful not to tear its dry leathery base, he mounted it among the others. There were brunettes, red heads, curly ones and straight, but mostly blonds, mostly blonds.

He smiled and reassured them. "Aw now, don't be jealous. I love *all* my little ladies."

Maneuvering his way through the forest of spiraling ponytails, stroking them as he passed, he headed out back.

Chapter 1

I was so sure of myself, thought I had it all figured out. I realized only too late I was nothing but a child, that we're all children in the eyes of God.

Disillusionment is a bitch. The scales were ripped from my eyes; not a hint of innocence was left in me, perhaps not even from a celestial perspective.

This is how it happened, so many years ago:

In a fortress, the walls that protect also imprison. It's pitch dark here, and the space never-ending, yet I can hear myself breathing.

A call from the void sooths me. But something isn't right. The voice beckons from across a great divide, an abyss within which something unthinkable lurks. I know this, but I don't remember how *I know it.*

I trust the voice, yet it asks of me something I cannot give.

I can't. I won't.

At least not today, the day of my arrival.

Today I will just survive.

Today is—

Wednesday, September 8th, the day before the first day of school in Morrilton, Arkansas. The town was large enough to scrape together a few Little League baseball teams, but small enough no one bothered locking up when they left home. In fact, this time of year, doors and windows remained open throughout the night, in hopes of a visit from the good witch of the Ozarks. She arrives in silence, curtains dancing on the ghostly breeze, in her wake the lullaby song of a whippoorwill, an effective remedy for even the worst of insomniacs.

Cities are human termite mounds, teeming with tumult, people packed like crayons into brick and metal boxes. Tempers flaring, horns blaring, each set of eyes regards the next with suspicion if not contempt.

The suburbs offer little respite; shouts of neighbors bleed through the walls, the space between houses little more than the width of a lawn mower. Deadbolts batten every door. Windows are locked and shades are drawn. Fences shout, *What's yours is yours, what's mine is mine, back off!*

On the outskirts of Morrilton, each home sits in isolation, nestled in acres of woods. Squirrels and the occasional deer offer twitching ears and watchful eyes—but no replies. Craving companionship, passing motorists share a toot and a wave. Church is crowded and trips into town turn into gossip gatherings.

A tin-roofed market of complaining plank floors and dangling bug-bulbs had supplied Morrilton with all it needed—produce and bait, beer and bacon—

since before the first car had come rattling down the dirt road, farting filth and scaring off the game. Called simply *The Market,* or *Neighbors'* (after its owner, "Lucky" Neighbors), the store had never been officially named—or licensed or advertised or painted or air-conditioned. After Lucky's passing, his kids sold out, packed up, and moved on to bigger and better things.

No larger than a city super service station, the new Piggly Wiggly was nevertheless to some a shining castle on a hill, a point of town pride, a seed of welcome progress. To others, it was an intrusive concrete complex, a sign of the times, a death knell to what Morrilton once had been.

It was 9:45 p.m., nearly closing time. Remnants of chatter still hung in the air—and the slap of kids' bare feet, and the ghosts of their laughter. Only two of tonight's patrons remained in the store.

Jessi Owen, valedictorian of her fourth-grade class, stood arms crossed in retro bell-bottom jeans adorned with embroidered butterflies. She glared down at her mother, who seemed unable to grasp the fact that *fifth grade starts tomorrow!* "Mom. The store's closing." She shifted her weight from one leg to the other. "Why are we looking at ice cream when we haven't even been to the school-supplies department yet?"

Grace Owen squatted at the cooler, brow knitted in concentration. "Sweetie, ten feet of pegboard tucked away in the dog-food aisle hardly constitutes a department." She donned similar jeans, sans the butterflies, and a white t-shirt advertising nothing. "We could fuss and fidget with ever' pencil and notebook over there and still be done by yesterday."

Jessi sighed dramatically.

Grace turned to her with a sly smile. "Why don't we just skip school tomorrow, Jess? Lay around all day eatin' ice cream. Whaddaya say?"

"*What?*" Jessi planted her fists on her hips. "I, for one, want to get an education."

Grace shrugged. "All I ever needed was horse sense."

"Mom. Have you ever seen a horse in college?"

"Never been to college. But I seen a mule eat a man's hat one time."

"Mom!"

"Well have you ever seen anything but a smile on the face of two girls eatin' ice cream?" She raised her eyebrows.

"Master Pastor says ice cream's full of fat and sugar."

"Well honey, if I'm gonna eat somethin' bad for me, it might as well be something I like."

Jessi groaned as she slung her ponytail and headed for school supplies on her own. She'd grown old enough to somewhat understand this little schooling-vs-common-sense game they played, so she stormed away resisting a grin.

Grace gazed after her, watching as she turned the corner. "Go get 'em, girl." The slightest tremor edged her voice when she added, "And don't you never look back."

She shifted her attention to the cooler again, and her crafty smile returned. *Chocolate almond or choco-*

late chip cookie dough? Her eyeless reflection looked like a ghost.

— —

Double chocolate fudge or dark chocolate? Which was it, damn it?

Master Pastor, who was neither a master nor a pastor, hated it when his wife Vivian ran off without her cell phone. But now he'd forgotten his. So he had a fifty-fifty shot at retrieving the correct brownie mix, at stake the inevitable inquiry, *Well, if you weren't sure, why didn't you just call?*

A chuckle escaped him. *Vigilant! Aware! Cat-like reflexes!* Some master you are, pastor.

Speaking of aware, he'd also failed to notice the steadily intensifying smell of ozone in the air, and an almost imperceptible rumble cascading over the hills. *Should have grabbed an umbrella.*

His nickname was born of the fact that Devin James was both pastor of Morrilton Baptist Church (though he was unordained) and taught Taekwondo in the narthex at night (though his rank was below that of a master).

Master Pastor. Both. Neither.

Most folks considered this an odd mix of life pursuits. But in Devin's mind, they were practically the same. He drew on his martial arts experience to illustrate spiritual concepts in his sermons, and he found the mat as fertile a sowing-ground for the seeds of enlightenment as the church.

He pulled into the Piggly Wiggly parking lot. He had his choice of spaces. He reached for the door release, but didn't pull it. His hand hovered over the handle. He sat staring out the window at the SUV sitting two slots over in the lamplight.

The Owens. Grace and Jessi.

The tang of disinfectant hid a trace of stale urine. Unintelligible, a voice crackled from the overhead speakers out in the hall. Wilted flower arrangements crowded a table in the corner. Mike Owen looked like he'd endured a decade's stay on a treeless island, a shriveled wisp of the man he once had been. Thin clear-plastic hoses wormed into his veins by way of needles secured with Betadine-stained tape.

His hand was a dead fish, weak in Devin's grip. "You're more than just a teacher to her, you know."

"Of course." Devin forced a smile. "I'm a first-rate Taekwondo instructor."

"You're more like her uncle. Even a fa . . . " His chin quivered and he looked away.

"Don't talk like that. You'll be up and outta here in—"

"This ain't no time for denials, preacher."

Devin's face felt hot. The room seemed to shrink.

"Promise me you'll—"

"You know you don't have to ask."

Mike somehow found the strength to raise his head and squeeze Devin's hand like a table vice. "Promise me." His fierce gaze seemed to melt his jaundiced irises.

Devin slowly nodded. His vision clouded.

"Please. I need to hear you say it, Devin."

He steeled himself with a deep breath. "I promise, Mike. By God I promise."

Mike's hand relaxed. His head fell back on the pillow and his eyes eased shut. "Now look at you." With some effort, he conjured a smile. "A man o' the cloth, taking the Lord's name in vain."

He studied his lap, the dashboard, the storefront. With a sigh, he set his jaw, hopped out, and headed toward the store.

Unseen, dead leaves danced across the pavement, rattling like miniature skeletons. A breeze tousled his hair. Jogging toward the entrance, he inhaled the pungent ozone. He marveled at the fascination, the excitement laced with fear, the primal dread and longing of the calm before a storm.

〜 〜

"Sensei!" Jessi bolted from the checkout counter, nearly knocked Devin over with a hug. Before he could return it, she pulled away. "Guess what?"

"What?"

"I learned Sip Jin this afternoon. Wanna know how?"

"How?" A grin stole around his ear.

"By watching the CDs you gave me!"

A laugh—born of love and pride but a laugh none-theless—tried to bubble over. He tightened his lips and nodded approval. "I see someone has been using her spare time wisely. Why am I not surprised?"

She bobbed on her toes and clasped her hands. Devin wondered if she even realized she was doing it.

Grace Owen caught up, rolling a buggy. Jessi turned, paused a beat, then dug into the cart. "And look at my school supplies!"

"Evenin', Master Pastor." Grace nodded, holding his gaze. Her eyes belied her strained smile. Losing a husband was not for sissies. Nor was losing a father.

Jessi seemed oblivious of the wordless conversation that passed between the grownups. She handed Devin a spiral notebook from the cover of which a cartoon girl threw a side kick at him. "Mom got it for me even though it cost more than the regular ones." She pronounced the last word *oneth*.

Devin studiously ignored it. "Whoa. That is some side kick." She'd been working hard to fix her lisp, and only let one slip occasionally. While he was proud of her efforts, he hated to see it go. One day—sooner than he would like—he'd turn to her, only to find himself facing a grown woman with a life of her own.

Grace sighed, eyes on her daughter, evidently plagued by the same sentiments.

Devin returned the notebook. "Better hurry if I'm going to beat the storm." He tipped an imaginary hat— "Ladies." —and turned to go.

Jessi shouted after him. "See you on the mat, Master Pastor!"

Devin waved and smiled over his shoulder, headed for the baking aisle.

— —

As Grace bagged her final items, the heavens opened up. The initial drops snapped on the pavement, followed almost instantly by skeins of rain, alien weaving ghost-giants aglow in the halogen parking lot lights.

Becca Hart, manager and sole employ for the night, turned to the glass storefront. "I hope you girls didn't leave your windows down." In her mid-fifties, padded with a few extra pounds, she waddled on arthritic knees.

Grace sighed, then crossed her arms and leaned against the counter to wait out the worst of it.

"Come on, Mom!" Jessi from the pneumatic doors. They'd already slid open.

"Jessi!" Grace hefted herself from the counter. Too late. The girl had ducked squealing into the torrents, blue jean jacket pulled over her head.

Grace's shoulders fell. She shook her head and turned to Becca Hart. "Do you have something I can put over these school supplies?"

"This oughtta do it." She'd already fished an umbrella from behind the checkout stand. "Just bring it back next time."

"Thanks, Mrs. Hart." Grace paused at the door, opened the umbrella, then turned back to Becca. She shrugged— "Kids." —and took off into the parking lot, buggy rattling, loosing squeals of her own.

≈ ≈

Jessi bounded through rivulet-rivers and took wing over puddle-oceans. She rounded the SUV, slowing her roll to avoid slipping. Even as the locks disengaged via the remote, she realized her mistake.

She shouldn't have run so far from her mother.

She should have paid attention to her surroundings.

She knew all the stranger-danger rules, even taught them to younger kids in class. But they were just something you memorized to get your next belt, weren't they? They were actually for other kids, the ones in Master Pastor's lectures. Not for her; not really.

Because Mom would always protect her. Mom had it all under control. And if anyone ever messed with them, Master Pastor would kick their butts. He could kick *anyone's* butt. Not that he'd ever need to. This was Morrilton, not New York City.

A figure stood between the cars. Blotting out the lamplight. Big as Dad used to be, maybe bigger. Jessi's breath kicked up a notch, like before she entered a tournament ring.

His shadow made ink of the puddle in which she stood. Hooded, silhouetted to her, his face was a black hole. He wore a dark longcoat. Oil-stained hands dripped at his sides.

A funny feeling rose in her chest, like ants warming up for a footrace. They crept into her arms and legs, now her hands and feet, tiny legs skittering.

Maybe this was some Master Pastor prank. Like to demonstrate what could happen if you strayed too far off on your own. If that was the case, Sensei was sure making his point.

Or, still as the figure was standing, maybe it wasn't a man at all. Maybe it was just a dummy, a Halloween display some store clerk unloaded and forgot to bring in or something.

He lunged.

The wheels of Grace's brain froze up, refused to spin as fast as she needed them to. Every drop of rain seemed to fall through molasses. She demanded that she snap out of it, back to real time, back to reality. But even her legs came to a halt, all on their own, heedless of her orders to keep walking. She stood staring through the pouring rain.

The car. It hadn't been there when they'd parked. Strange-looking, perhaps an antique. That in itself was no big deal—until she considered the man in the longcoat. A Goliath, well over six feet tall. Of course surely he was harmless. Big, yes, but harmless. The father of one of Jessi's classmates. Surely.

Her heart thudded in her ears, unheeding of her assurances.

Why was Jessi just standing there? Did she not realize the SUV was open? Had the rain drowned out the clunking of the locks? The chirp of the alarm?

Her skin turned to gooseflesh.

The man lunged.

Without warning, the world zipped by in fast-forward, *too* fast, the raindrops a blur; her heart tumbled, hurdling down the runway like the space shuttle Challenger, disintegrating as it crashed and burned.

She dropped the umbrella, shoved the buggy aside and bolted into the downpour.

= =

Jessi grunted under her breath, struggling in vain to wrench free of the pit bull grip.

Yell for help!

That was number one on Master Pastor's list of simple self-defense weapons. *When you yell, the real weapon is the help it brings.*

Jessi got it, but Sensei had warned her this was easier said than done. Sure enough, the scream lodged in her throat and refused to break free.

Her forearm went numb; her pinkie tingled. *He's digging into my ulnar nerve.* The funny bone is not a bone at all, but a nerve—the largest in the human body unprotected by muscle or bone. How funny she should think of that at a time like this.

The freak's coat flapped open like a dragon wing. Across his chest in block letters, *Machine Man*. He was a machine alright, a hell-tractor on overdrive—a dozer, a forklift, a kid-harvesting combine—yanking her around like a rag doll.

Master Pastor's voice cut through the haze, a flicker of reason on a sea of panic: *In self-defense, the fight is never fair. Count on your attacker outweighing you by a ton. But you can play the* big-against-little *game, too. Instead of* big-hand-verses-small-hand, *think* sharp-teeth-verses-*tender*-hand.

That's right! The next line of defense was to *bite*. Bite anywhere, bite hard. You couldn't defeat a giant with your teeth, but you could sure get his attention.

Using both hands, Jessi did a chin-up on the crane-lift wrist. Using his grip instead of fighting it, she rode his arm, let her legs turn to rubber—her body to dead weight—then pressed her yawning mouth over the base of his thumb.

She clamped down with all her might. Her neck trembled. Her gums throbbed. She bit down harder still, shaking her head, growling like an angry schnauzer. She gagged when melted copper flooded her mouth.

He did not scream in pain, only jumped a little—and released her.

Rubber legs. She collapsed to her back. Her head smacked the pavement. She found herself staring through glowing ant races into Machine Man's upside-down ghost-face. He was examining his thumb, rain-swirled blood trickling down his wrist.

She rolled, shot-squirmed-scrambled for the SUV. Splashing like a hooked fish.

Her arm collapsed.

Oh yeah. Ulnar nerve.

She righted herself and tucked her arm to her tummy. Limped on all-threes. Knees throbbing, cheese-grated palm singing soprano. Her heart was a bunny foot thumping the earth. She heard herself chanting, *Un un un.*

She collapsed again, this time intentionally. Rolling for the shadows beneath the SUV. *Ever try fetching a cat from under a car, Mr. Muscle Man?*

He snared her ponytail. Yanked her from her hiding place. Incredibly, he lifted her. Strands ripping away at the roots. She latched onto his wrist with both hands, cooling the fire in her scalp.

He held her up and out, arm partially bent, an angled Heil Hitler.

Her foot lashed out. Disappeared into his hood. Struck something solid. She finally unleashed the pent-up scream.

His head snapped back; he stumbled.

Without the other foot grounded, her kick set her swinging.

She splashed once more to the pavement. Plopped onto her butt.

The freak backed off and raised his hands to his face. His hood fell back. Revealed beneath was a face like a Ken doll, only harder, like someone had ground his jaws into ax blades. She beetled her brow, shocked to discover he was handsome. Well, except for the silly mirrored shades hanging askew. And of course his gushing nose.

She shut her eyes and sucked in a breath. She found a calm cool center, even through the adrenaline, even through the pain, even through the tears she hadn't realized were flowing.

She opened her eyes.

Knitted her brow.

Ready to fight.

The Machine Man just stood there. Poised as if facing an opponent, but unmoving. Was he teasing her? Jessi was ready to either drop and roll or rise and fight—but the assault never came.

From above her rose a piercing shriek like an engine belt slipping.

Her mom sprang over her, primal scream, a machine herself. She plowed into the freak— "Jessi *run!*" —and started wailing on him. Her blows were untrained and ineffective, like a baby slapping a Hereford bull.

She knew her mom was right.

Sensei had talked about this. When the odds were overwhelming, the escape of one victim would at least ensure police assistance for the other—much more help than sitting tied up together in some backwoods hideaway.

But this was her *mom*.

She gritted her teeth and sprang up to join the fight—or to try and drag her mother away.

The man slammed Grace into the SUV. Drop-kicked Jessi in the chest. Lightning shot from her solar plexus to her spine, up her neck, around her skull and into her brain. She plummeted to the pavement. Whiplashed her neck. Her teeth jarred with the impact.

The pistol seemed to just magically appear. Like a gun you'd see on a movie poster. Jessi struggled to her feet, hugging her tummy, gasping for breath. Eyes locked on the gun.

Threaten us; that's what he'll do now. He'll show us who's boss, then rob us. It'll be scary, but the best show-n-tell story ever. I'll be the star of Taekwondo class.

She found herself sitting on a hardwood pew, butt long-since numbed. Listening in rapt silence. Master Pastor entranced the crowd from the pulpit: *"Make your peace with God, my friends. Not tomorrow, not tonight. Today. Do it* now.*" He wandered from behind the pulpit into the aisle.*

"You see, although death lingers always on the edge of our consciousness, it's visible only in our periphery. Even when we tease ourselves with thoughts of our own demise, we're never truly convinced it will happen." He smiled as he scanned the congregation. "Not really."

A cough echoed through the church, from maybe two rows behind her. "This strange ability to deny death's inevitable arrival keeps us sane. We proceed through life as if we're invincible, as if the cavalry will always come rumbling to the rescue at the penultimate moment." A baby complained; a mother quietly consoled it.

"And if violence is the horse upon which the hooded guest arrives, our very death-day could be blissful, right up to the moment the darkness turns to greet us."

Deafening thunder, fire like the lightning. Grace took two in the chest and slid limp down the SUV.

Jessi couldn't wrap her head around it. She couldn't breathe, couldn't feel her face. Her eyes locked on the gushing craters, on her mother lying broken in the rain. She remained frozen as the man stepped over the corpse, as he holstered the .45, even as he cocked his fist for a backhand blow.

Flash of light, and then the darkness.

— —

It was just a thunder clap. Or a backfire from an old pickup. Or a transformer blowing. That's what he told himself.

Devin stood staring over his left shoulder toward the front of the store. The brownie mix hovered before him as if he were trying to read the ingredients with his right ear.

Even if it had been gunfire, that didn't necessarily mean anything. Firearms were as common as hats in these small towns. So maybe someone had accidentally loosed a round.

Except it had been *two* rounds. And who would have a gun out fooling with it in this downpour? In the Piggly Wiggly parking lot? Past ten at night?

He blindly set the box on the shelf and started easing—now walking, now jogging—back toward the front. His pulse picked up, not from the exertion.

He rounded the last gondola. Slowed to a halt.

Becca Hart stood stock still in profile to him. Seemingly entranced. She held a broom in one hand, a dustpan in the other, positioned horizontally as if she'd just swept up a pile of gold dust.

He followed her gaze to the front doors, both of which stood open to the storm. Standing on the pressure mat, silhouetted in the halogen lights, a caped figure. Hooded. His black wing billowed in the wind, lashing the night.

Devin gasped. *A vampire?* But of course no bloodsucker would rise from its coffin wearing a *Machine Man* t-shirt.

Or carrying a pistol.

Once he processed it, the cape, the shirt, the hood—even the chrome plated .45—struck him as juvenile. Over-the-top. Just plain stupid. Yet his heart had scuttled into his throat, and he couldn't seem to swallow it.

Becca dropped the broom. Turned on her heel. For some reason, she retained the dustpan—one-handed, balanced before her like a serving platter as she bumbled away. To what safety did she think she could retreat? Why was she holding on to the dustpan? A crushing pity for the woman overcame him. The humiliation. The shock. Her stark fear.

Devin jumped in place a split second before he registered the blast. Becca Hart smacked the tile like a sack of flour. The dustpan careened across the floor, struck the checkout counter, spun in place for a beat then came to rest. He stared at the place she'd been standing, expecting her to pop back up like a Jack-in-the-box. *(I'm okay! I'm okay!)*

His throat bobbed. His knees turned to rubber.

He found himself gawking back at the doorway, his eyes begging of the vampire a silent one-word question.

The gunman lowered his hood. Smiled back at him. Devin had expected a ravaged visage twisted in rage. In fact, the face belonged on a Calvin Klein ad. Except for the blood goatee. And of course Calvin Klein didn't offer 1977 mirror-shades reminiscent of Smokey and the Bandit.

Machine Man raised the .45. Still smiling. The men locked eyes over the sites of the pistol.

Devin suddenly remembered the correct brownie mix. Vivian had said, *Dark chocolate's got that bite to it, like a hint of espresso.*

Crazy.

The gunman held out his arms and bobbed his head once. "News common sense—"

News common sense? Did he mean common sense news?

"—RUN!"

Devin sent a flee command to his feet. Before the message arrived, thunder rattled the windows and hammered his eardrums. The shot took him in the ribs. Right under the left pec. Lava squirted into his spine—his arms, his neck. He gasped in vain for breath. The world spun out of control.

Someone clubbed the back of his head. A panicked shopper shoving past? A second assailant? Vision closing to a pin-hole, he raised his hand to block a second assault, turned to see who had hit him and discovered it was the floor.

The lights faded. Deafening buzz.
Darkness.

— —

Machine Man set to work prepping for departure. He needed to leave as much time as possible before the discovery of—and response to—the clusterfuck that had just happened here.

He cut the phone line in the front office. A 9-1-1 call was inevitable, but most of these ole boys didn't carry cell phones, so the investment in time possibly to delay that call was worth it.

The poor bastard he'd blown clean off his feet lay far enough back to be well out of sight—at least from a casual glance through the windows.

He dragged the old lady by her feet, left her behind the checkout counter. He plucked the keys from her smock. He decided to leave the blood. No one would recognize it for what it was in the darkness—if they even saw it at all. He hustled to the exit and turned out the lights, then locked the doors as he left.

He jogged to the SUV, fished the keys from the feisty skank's pocket (She didn't have no purse. What kinda uppity bitch didn't carry no purse?) and opened the tailgate. He stuffed her inside. Slammed it shut. Locked her in there. The corpse mingled with the shadows, impossible to see 'less you cupped your hands to the glass.

The rain had sluiced away the bloody puddle.

He folded into his car, slammed the door, then twisted the key in the ignition. The engine rumbled to life.

He needed to skedaddle, like, yesterday. It would be morning before any alarm was raised, so if he left in a hurry, he'd be miles from here and done with his business by then.

He didn't move. Because not six feet behind him, dozing peacefully in the trunk, lay his Sleeping Beauty. He shuddered with anticipation. He gazed into the rear-view, almost expecting to find her smiling back at him from the rear seat.

He shook his head and threw the car in gear.

He couldn't afford a delay, no sir. But Goddamn he wanted to ask her *now!*

Is it you? Are you the one?

Not yet . . . Not yet.

= =

Master Pastor cringed a little when people referred to martial arts as a sport. Because it was so much more than that. For Devin James, martial arts was a way of life. While learning, practicing, and teaching combat techniques delighted him, what hooked him were the life-lessons that so readily presented themselves in training. A tough class was like a mirror reflecting one's inner nature. Of course, making the changes necessary to perfect that nature was up to the practitioner.

There seemed to be two approaches to martial arts training: *Grow Your Spirit* or *Hone Technique.* He'd found that if your practice didn't address both, it addressed neither.

His job at the church kept him thinking, kept him always on his toes. He'd been corralled into filling in when the preacher had disappeared, mysteriously on the same day the choir director's wife had left him. Devin had enjoyed the experience more than expected. So had the congregation. And so after one substitute Sunday became two—then many—an unspoken agreement was reached that he would serve as the pastor indefinitely.

His preference was counseling, because the pulpit challenged him. His messages were unorthodox though reliably interesting, often peppered with analogies from the martial arts life. His parishioners referred to him as Master Pastor as frequently as did his Taekwondo students.

He read incessantly. Michael Crichton, Dean Koontz—anything sophisticated and thrilling. And of course his bible. Not because it gave him peace. To the contrary, he'd yet to figure it out. He worked the verses like a crossword puzzle, straining to see what others saw, or claimed to see, straining to *understand.*

Devin James carried his bible with him everywhere he went. He was more likely to forget his wallet (or cell phone) than his Good Book. It rumpled his jackets, about which he could have cared less. He kept it always tucked away in his left inside pocket.

Today was no exception.

In the front cover, a charred hole about the diameter of a first grade pencil matched the one in his coat. The hole grew toward the back, singeing paper as it swelled. Mangled in the final burnt pages of Revelation, gleaming on the back cover, a flattened chunk of lead. Behind the destroyed book, two of his ribs throbbed. Badly bruised and probably broken.

Rattling. Shuffling. His vision faded and resolved as if a monkey were fiddling with the focus controls. His head rolled lazily on the tile.

Footsteps. Someone stirring busily.

The lights blinked out. *(Am I conscious?)* Keys jingling, lock turning . . . Becca closing up?

No, not Becca.

Jessi!

His eyes snapped open. He bolted upright—then immediately fell back. He almost screamed in pain, but traded it for a muted snarl.

He fingered under his jacket—touched his ribs—snatched his hand away wincing.

Gotta get up. Gotta move. *Now!*

Grunting, grimacing, he struggled to his feet. Staggered forward.

Lean on the checkout counter—that's it—now the office-door facing—rest a second—okay, let's go.

He snatched up the phone. Held it to his ear. Silence. He rattled the button in the cradle.

The muted thud of a car door. He glanced at the wall, almost expecting his vision to penetrate the painted concrete.

Police?

No sirens. Not that lucky.

He dropped the receiver. Stumbled to the office door. Leaned on the frame and gasped for breath. Doubled over, hugging his ribs, he troll-walked five steps—and stuttered to a stop.

Becca Hart lay face down on the cold tile. Arms stretched over her head. Smock gathered at her armpits. Her hands had painted smears on the floor. Her hair was a paintbrush, dipped in red.

"Mrs. Hart?" His voice cracked. He expected no answer and received none.

He groaned as he forced himself upright, spittle spraying from between clinched teeth. He limped to the door. Expecting it to magically open like always—*BAM!*—he walked right into it.

Pain. Still in his ribs, now in his head—and growing in his heart.

Nausea.

Choke it down. *Breathe.*

Headlights fanned the parking lot, then a car followed them down the exit lane.

The gunman. Had to be.

The Owens had just been leaving. And the first shots had come from out there.

He had to know, had to *see*.

The doors were keyed on both sides—no thumb latch.

Back door?

Too slow.

Strange taillights—over-sized, slanted in a *V*—eased left out of the parking lot onto South Bridge

Road. His heart slammed at his aching ribs. He suddenly felt lightheaded. He slapped his palms against the glass— *"No!"* —entreating the lights to *listen*. To stop. To come back to him.

His hands balled into fists. His upper lip twitched. He retreated three steps. Focused on the doors. He skipped sideways, almost backwards toward the glass—and kicked with his heel.

The doors rumbled but held firm. Clawing at his ribs, he tried again, this time stepping and spinning backwards 180 degrees with reckless disregard for accuracy or his pain.

The glass shattered, a sparkling constellation in the storm.

He ran to the SUV. Ribs on fire. The rain revitalized him, cleared his head a little. He cupped his hands to his mouth. "Grace!" He bent to the passenger window, peered inside.

Nothing.

He stood. *"Jessi!"*

Back seat. Empty.

He scanned the parking lot. Empty.

He strode to the back of the SUV. Staring through the rear window, through the tunnel that was his own cupped hands, his breath caught in his throat. He heard himself keening.

He pushed away. Turned in circles. Laced his fingers in his hair. He tilted his face up into the pounding rain, blinking at the droplets. He asked of God what he'd silently asked the killer.

Of course there was no reply. There never was.

He lowered his head. Propped his hands on his knees. Spat on the pavement.

After a beat, he dropped to one knee and peered under the SUV. No Jessi. He stood, cupped his hands to his mouth again. Bellowed her name. The storm swallowed his voice.

Again, louder, ribs searing . . . Only the torrents answered his call.

He glanced down the road. The taillights had faded to pinpoints.

No cell phone.

No landline.

No help.

Come on, think—*Think!*

If Jessi were hiding somewhere, she'd be traumatized but okay without him. But if she were in that car . . .

He ran to the minivan and vaulted inside. Started the engine. Slammed it in gear. The van nearly tipped peeling out of the parking lot.

The lights had disappeared around a bend in the road a good mile south. If they made another turn . . .

He floored it, muffled engine roar, valves pinging. Rain streaked up the windshield in defiance of gravity. Shuddering like it was, it felt like the chassis might disintegrate.

By habit, Devin glanced in the rearview, hoping to find an empty street, or at least one free of flashing blue lights. Then again, blue lights might be a good thing.

He scanned the area for a cruiser, perhaps hiding behind hedges or nestled in a parking space.

On the other hand, if they pulled him over, one of two things would happen: They'd believe his story and give pursuit immediately, or they'd hold him for questioning until it could be verified. He had no trouble guessing the most likely scenario.

"Come on, catch up. *Catch up!*"

But then what?

Confronting the gunman would no doubt be met with deadly force. Devin was unarmed. Dead, he would do Jessi no good.

He'd just have to close the gap and play it by ear.

Without warning, his temper boiled over. "She's just a *kid!*" The featureless face to whom he spoke had ears but no voice. The Old Man had His Big Agenda, and He didn't make deals.

Devin offered one anyway. "Take me." His breath kicked up; he started to panic. Though prayers for riches and rainless Saturdays reliably went unanswered, sure as shit this one would be granted. Had he spoken too soon? How would Vivian take his request? Would she be hurt? Feel betrayed? No, she'd understand.

He spoke again, probably to nothing but the dashboard. "You tell us to pray for Your will, but to make our desires known. To just ask." He gritted his teeth, twisting at the wheel. "Well *I'm asking.*"

The best scenario would be that they both survived, that he'd mentor Jessi to mastery, that he'd one day play Mr. Miyagi to her children. But he knew it didn't work like that. He knew somewhere along the road, the gatekeeper would demand a toll of blood.

Chapter 2

This place must be Nowhere. What else could it be?

Friends accompany me here—eyes like a doll's eyes, painted faces. I try to converse, but their replies are plastic. Phony. They say what I expect them to say.

With only them as company, I will surely go insane.

But the voice is real. *I know this not by evidence but by faith. Funny how the faceless voice is the only one I trust. Maybe I'm already insane, these phony friends the whole ones.*

Or maybe I'm dead.

The abyss: I have seen what awaits me there, but I dare not remember. I dare not look at it or speak its name.

The voice again; I approach the precipice. The ghosts wail and moan, more tormented with each step I take. Some tear at themselves and one another, weeping and gnashing their teeth. Senseless whispers.

The voice reaches out to me, calming me, reassuring me.

Deceiving me?

My eyes fall.

I gasp.

There! Glowing red eyes stared back at Devin through the endless night, mocking him. Slanted, uncharacteristically large—must be an antique or something.

They were turning off South Bridge onto the Old Conway Highway. The road ran east, snaked through Clinton into Conway, then farther into Oak Grove and beyond. An endless, unlit, two-lane highway, it ran for miles through dense woods, splitting sprawling cotton fields and painting a black stripe through each small town it passed. It eventually veered south and became Woodson Lateral, which cut a groove through the Arkansas hills, sometimes going by other aliases, eventually slithering its way to the southern Arkansas border and beyond.

Devin had caught up just a few miles south of the store, but he'd kept his distance. When the road became hilly with tortuous curves, he'd closed in some, afraid of losing them. Concerned he may alert the driver to his tail, he fell back—too far back—then panic set in when he thought he'd lost them for good. He was no James Bond; tailing someone was new to him. Now, just in time to see the eyes make this crucial turn, he'd finally relocated them.

He sighed with relief and relaxed his shoulders. He winced when his ribs complained.

But *them?* The hideous taillights, one-of-a-kind, left little doubt this was the same vehicle. The gunman's car. But he couldn't be certain Jessi was in it.

She'd failed to answer his call at the Piggly Wiggly, but this could have several explanations: The deafening rain, for one. Or she could have been hiding behind a dumpster or in the nearby woods, scared to death and unwilling or unable to respond. Or maybe she'd fled, had run until her legs collapsed.

That was the response he recommended to a violent attack: *Escape!* He prayed that's what she'd done—but betting on it would be foolish. Of course, God forbid, she could be lying dead in the freak's trunk, which would mean Devin was risking his life for nothing. He tried not to think about that.

The most prudent course of action seemed to be to follow the car and further assess the situation when he was able. They'd eventually have to stop somewhere. He could use a payphone or borrow a cell to contact the authorities and that would be the end of it.

He droned down the Old Conway Highway, under the distant gaze of the slanted eyes. The slapping of the windshield wipers was a hypnotist's pendulum, lulling him, taking him back.

The Tape.

Digging through some old videotapes a few years back, he'd stumbled across footage of a great match. The winner had possessed such grace and poise, such blinding speed and devastating power. Devin had sat transfixed, shaking his head in awe. At the end of the match, the other guy lay cold on the mat.

A tinge of jealously bit at him. Okay, more than a tinge. He outright resented the guy. *Why can't I fight like that?*

As the video drew to an end, the P.A. squealed—then the announcer boomed, "In ring four, Devin James wins by knock out!" Stunned stupid, brow furled, he rewound the tape. Had he heard right? He'd competed so frequently that the venues all looked the same. Distance and camera angle—and of course the sparring gear—disguised all facial features. But upon closer examination, the announcer was proven correct. The mystery fighter was indeed he himself, Devin James. Jubilant, heart pounding, he'd watched the match again.

And again and again.

It was gone. He never recovered the envy—or even an ounce of appreciation—for the fighter that was now himself, for the skill he'd witnessed right there on the tape.

That turn was slow, that roundhouse too low.

You dropped your guard.

You won by sheer luck when he walked right into your hook kick.

Hot tears of frustration burned his eyes, threatening to break the seal.

It had been there. The skill, the speed, the power. He'd *seen* it! So why couldn't he see it *now?*

Only anger would stay the tears. He banged the eject button, nearly knocking over the player. Yanked out the cartridge. Stormed outside to the trash barrel. He stood holding the lid open for a full minute.

He tore the brown strip from the casing, again and again—until he clamped in his fist an eagle's nest of magnetic tape. He ripped even that to pieces, then dropped it all in and slammed the lid.

God had offered a mirror, a rare chance to see himself as others saw him. But the image therein somehow vexed him. Vivian tried, his instructor tried, everyone tried. But he was simply unable to appreciate himself.

He'd heard somewhere that God sometimes burdens one soul in the process of—even for the purpose of—blessing another. The love forbidden to himself he instead showered on his students. He preached self-confidence and self-respect, insisted on it. People loved him for that. And he loved the joyous noise that drowned out the cry for help from within himself.

The left taillight flickered. He squinted and watched. No, not an effect of the drizzle. Not the turn signal, either. Too intermittent. The bulb burning out? Maybe—but it didn't really act like that. It shimmered and shook, distorted through the trickles on the windshield. Then the whole fixture seemed to shift positions, to move a little.

What the . . .

Devin closed in as much as he dared. The rain was dying, but without street lamps, he worried about losing them with no taillights to track.

Nothing happened for half a minute; he nearly backed off. Maybe he'd imagined it.

Then it did something he couldn't have imagined.

He laughed aloud and shook his head. The mystery of the curiously blinking taillight was solved.

＝ ＝

There! Headlights again.

Damn. Maybe they was different ones from back in Morrilton, but he sure shit wouldn't bet on it. Johnny Law? Probably not. Least not one that knew about the Piggly Wiggly. If they did, they'd be hightailing it after him. Probably just some hayseed driving back to his little jerkwater town.

Just watch him and keep it under the speed limit. Colt's on the seat.

Machine Man.

That was the nickname ole coach Tanner had give Tim Loveless. Way back in high school. Didn't take a lot of imagination; he'd wore his black t-shirt with the words blasted across his chest in big block letters almost ever' day. But Coach Tanner always claimed he moved like a mindless meat machine on the football field, so it sure fit.

"Machine Man" was his favorite song by his favorite band, *Ellis D. and the Alter Egos.* He looked like ole Ellis too, even still today. Six-four, chiseled face, 240 pounds—and he'd got his self some combat boots and a black oiled-leather longcoat just like the singer's. He topped it off with mirrored "D" shades. Wore 'em every day, even at night.

Badass, oh yes he was.

Once, some head-beaters and blow-hards in the marching band had thought his outfit looked funny. Snickered at him. *That's okay, that's alright.* Why, he'd just bided his time 'til one night he come barreling over the sideline like a Goddamn freight train and planted his helmet right in one o' their fat little faces.

Now that was funny!

Back in the day, he'd been able to lay waste to any dipstick on that field. Once he uppercut a front lineman, right behind his face guard. Jacked him up high in the air—then he hit the grass, flat on his ass. Kid broke two teeth biting through his mouthpiece. Had to haul him off in a neck brace. Only problem was, Tim got throwed out the game for it!

Back on the sidelines, coach Tanner had smacked him upside the helmet. "N' use common sense, boy! Next time you want to do something like that, make sure the ref ain't looking."

Damn he loved football.

'Course, there was a time ole Tim his self got jacked up. Jacked up good.

Wasn't nothing he could do about it.

'Cause they all bitches.

Thump. Tim checked the rearview.

Were the damn old speakers about to bust? The backseat woofer seemed to be turning inside-out or something. The old hag owned this piece of shit probably never had the volume turned loud enough to hear—'less you stuck your damn head in the speakers. They're bitches when they're old. Bitches when they're young, too.

Hell, they're bitches ever' one, cradle to grave.

Who gives a shit about the speakers? Won't need the car much longer anyway.

But there it went again. Hell, maybe it was a tire going flat.

Or maybe Little Mary was startin' to stir. He turned down ole Ellis and listened.

Nothing.

Probably the speakers. Just watch the volume.

He turned it back up.

Girls.

"I love 'em, but I hate 'em," he said aloud. He'd been bitten alright, oh yes he had.

But just you remember, like ole Ellis D. says:

I'll be comin' back, with a vengeance!

And back I come, didn't I? And speak this ole machine did, didn't it? Oh yes it did.

The drone of the road took him back in time. He visited the practice field . . . Ms. McGrooter's English class . . . the high school machine shop. Faces of girls resolved and faded, and cars and fights and mangled joints ironed flat from riding his pocket all day.

He floated back further still, where Handle hovered before him.

Just a old ax handle; his Daddy had give it to him. Well, didn't really *give* it to him; he just chunked it after he changed it out, and Timmy wrestled it out the trash pile. But Daddy didn't say nothing, so he kind of gave it to him.

Timmy tested the weight of the stick. It felt good in his hands, like magic power leeched from the wood into his skin.

He glanced around the yard. The truck windshield caught his eye. His backside burned just thinking about it. Same with the light-globe over the door.

He just needed to try it out, so he strode over to the big elm out front not twenty feet from the trailer. The base was nearly big around as the truck bed. He turned his eyes skyward, up high into the canopy. Squinting. He shaded his eyes with his free hand. Squirrels played in the branches up there, silhouettes frolicking in spokes of light. Legions of leaves twisted and turned in waves like a chorus of angels whispering on the breeze.

Timmy smiled. He returned his gaze to his target, blinked sunspots from his eyes. He hefted the handle, paused a beat—then brought it down. The *thud* jarred his wrists. Shook his spine. It hurt, but it kind of felt good, too.

He brought it down again. This time a spray of bark excited him. And a trickle of sap was like amber blood, trickling down into the dirt. He stood watching it, expressionless—for a good full minute.

He resumed the pounding.

After some time, he registered the truck pulling in. He hadn't even heard it leave.

(Thud. Thud.)

The engine died. The door squeaked on its hinges, slammed shut.

(Thud. Thud.)

He was soaked in sweat. His hands ached. Warm slickness on his palms. Blood? Busted blisters?

(Thud. Thud.)

Footsteps. Crunching gravel—now mashing the grass.

Keep walking. Please just keep on walking.

The footsteps came to a halt behind him, at the foot of the rickety rusted steps. A paper bag rustled. Crack of a beer tab. "Boy, what the hell you think you're doing?" The old man's vocal chords were marinated in alcohol, basted in pot smoke.

Timmy paused, panting. But he didn't look back. "Gonna kill it." He realized he was standing in a shadow, a gray ghost hiding in the grass now revealed. The revenant raised a shadow hand, in the hand a shadow can. Gulps from behind him sounded like boots tromping through mud, or a goat being strangled.

Then a belch. "That is some seriously fucked up, faggoty-ass shit." Silence . . . then a sizzle: A cigarette coal being sucked to life. Reeking smoke billowed around him.

"Faggot."

Timmy gritted his teeth and squeezed his eyes shut.

"Sissy."

A shove from behind sent him stumbling a step. His eyes shot open. He snarled.

"Gone cry?"

His breath kicked up.

"Gone cry now?" Gus Loveless put on a whiny tone: "Boo hoo. What'll I do."

Timmy twisted his hands on the handle.

"Go on, try it."

Trembling.

"I'll break it over your damn head and fuck you with it." Another sizzle of the cigarette. "Oh yes I will."

Half a minute passed.

The steps complained. Once, twice, thrice. "Wash my truck—" The screen door whined. "—sissy." The footsteps faded. *(Robin! What the hell'd I tell you about . . .)* The old man's voice trailed away.

Timmy raised the stick again, then brought it crashing down.

They hit it off good, him and Handle. People came and went, but ole Handle was always there. Celebrated his victories. Consoled him in defeat. Sometimes in his dreams, it spoke to him. He could never remember what it said, but come morning he always felt better. Relaxed. *Powerful.* He carried his friend with him everywhere he went.

Out to the junkyard, any rat dumb enough to come bumbling out was taken by a swing like Babe Ruth plowing one over center field.

He ran to the quivering corpse. "Take that!" *Whack.* "And that!" *Whack.* "And that, and that, and that!" *Whack.* He wasn't sure what "that" was for, but it was certainly something.

One night, the howl of a cat dragged him from his dreams. Ole Handle beckoned from the corner, whispering in the moonlight.

Daddy was on a bender, wouldn't wake up 'til tomorrow afternoon.

Mama slept like the dead.

He slipped out of bed, snared his Excalibur, and tiptoed out the door.

Handle.

A ole possum come to call. Damn thing looked like a overgrown rat.

Handle.

Raccoons in the garbage.

Handle.

A garter snake under the trashcan.

Handle.

A nest of twigs and strips of twine, squirming pink bundles snuggled within, trembling beaks wide-open . . .

He finally killed the tree, too.

Eventually.

Fourth grade: *"BEND OVER!"* Every kid's eyes turned to Ms. Hackett. Today was no different than any other day; she shouted it *every* day, more than once on most days.

They called her paddle "Gentle Ben," so named because her battle cry sounded like *Ben Dover!* Although only in her early thirties, her scowl—and sadistic temper, and acne-scarred face, and voice like a rasp—aged her twenty years. They'd dubbed her *Old Battle Ax.* Of course, no kid uttered it within earshot.

There was a time when parents trusted teachers. If you got a paddling at school, you got another one at home. But as always seems to happen, corruption wormed its way into the system. Little Caesars with rotten hearts sated their hunger for power in the classroom. There would come a day when corporeal punishment was banned. In fact, the pendulum would swing the other way entirely, when even an unkind word spoken to a student would be grounds for a lawsuit, lest a teacher do irreparable psychological damage to an "addled youth" when calling him out for selling crack in science class.

But those days were yet to come, and the days of honorable educators long since past. These kids were caught in the transition.

Timmy cowered and braced himself—but he was not her target. Rather, classmate David Beach had earned her wrath. The poor bastard made the mistake of giggling when Miss Hackett realized she'd forgot her paddle. This was a grave error in judgment and, too late, David realized his mistake. "I'm sorry! Please, Ms. Hackett. I—"

Because what Miss Hackett *did* have in her hand was a teacher's edition math book. She swung it at the boy's head, landed a glancing blow as he ducked. He wound up bent over his desk, his ear an angry red.

Miss Hackett jabbed a skeleton finger in his face— *"Stay there!"* —and hefted the book. Too weak to support it in one hand, and unable to achieve a suitable horizontal swing with two, she raised the text high above her head with both hands. She brought it down on his back, as close to his rump as she could get it, bending her body, throwing her weight into it.

Timmy gawked, loath to watch but unable to turn away. The book fell, fell again, and again and again. As the beating proceeded, he realized someone's fingers had tiptoed into his. He glanced at his hand, then up to her face.

He blinked.

Impossible.

Mary Maples.

His heart was a Tommy gun blasting bullets of panic.

Mary sat on a throne of candy and lace, atop mountains of marigolds, behind bastions of glass impenetrable to him—untouchable, unknowable, invisible to him except from a distance. Her knobby knees were a map of his world, perpetually adorned with scrapes and bruises. Freckles splashed across her nose, a speckled tale of beaches and backyard barbecues.

He realized he'd stopped breathing. He blinked again and drew a breath.

His eyes drifted to her ponytail. Blond and buoyant; he'd never seen anything like it. Furtively he watched whenever she walked, but especially when she ran. The bouncing-swinging-rippling of the silky fine filaments captivated him, confused him. The feeling was nice—yet scary somehow. Speaking to or even about Mary Maples was something that had never even crossed his mind.

And now here she was, fingers laced in his.

Her eyes flooded, begging him not to shrink away. David's screams forgotten, he felt himself slipping, falling into those precious pools, down and down, never to return. He gave himself away.

Later that semester: He hadn't washed his left hand for nearly a week. He couldn't eat. Sleep was a sly fox, stealing his eyes by day, eluding him at night. Handle gathered dust in the corner, all but forgotten.

But Mary didn't seem to have changed at all. Like she didn't even remember the hand-holding. Or maybe she did; he just couldn't tell.

Timmy watched her always, divining hidden signs and signals in her every word and gesture. But on the rare occasion she returned his glance, she just smiled and turned away, sometimes with a shy wave. And never did she sit by him at lunch . . . but then she aways sat at the girls' table, so maybe that didn't mean nothing.

One day, he decided to just gut it on up and talk to her.

Mary was cleaning the hamster cage. She glanced up when Timmy arrived, then resumed her work.

He heard himself say, "Uh. Hi Mary."

"Well hello there, Timmy." She scraped a scoop of soiled cedar chips.

He didn't have much time; Old Battle Ax was on the prowl with Gentle Ben. "Uh. Do you like somebody?"

She creased her brow. "Why, I like everybody, silly." Her work slowed, her hands faltered.

Timmy shuffled his feet, trying to find the right words, trying to find the *courage*. "Uh, I mean, do you, like, *like* somebody?"

She sat down the hamster's water bottle. "Did someone put you up to this, Timmy Loveless?"

Put him up to this? What did she mean? That she liked him? That she didn't?

"Uh . . . yeah." No they hadn't. What was he *thinking?*

Girls.

She smiled and nodded. "Well, you tell *Mr. Mystery Boy* that 'Yes, I *do* like somebody,' and you tell him to meet me at the old oak tree at recess."

Then she winked at him.

Winked at him!

This had been easier than expected. *Mr. Mystery Boy.* He liked that. Come on, recess!

It didn't take him long to spot the shimmering ponytail. Mary seemed to be searching too, but hadn't seen him yet. She waved another direction, maybe at a girlfriend. She glanced over each shoulder. Looking for him. He waved, but she didn't see him.

She headed for the tree.

So did Timmy.

When Mary arrived, she took one final scan of the playground then slipped behind the oak. Timmy smiled and picked up the pace. As he neared, muted voices slowed his roll . . . then set his heart agallop.

Giggling.

From behind the tree.

Not just Mary.

He froze. His heart faltered like a bird shot dead mid-flight. Oh, he knew what it was. He knew. But he had to *see.* Keeping his distance, he slowly rounded the tree. Boys' raucous kickball-shouts faded into the distance. Screams of delight came from somewhere in a dream. His vision blurred.

Through the haze, the hem of her dress.

He circled farther.

Her ponytail.

He kept slowly circling.

Then her face, her sweet, sweet face. His Mary's face. *His* Mary's face.

Rapt in the eyes of another boy.

Damn Toby Thompson. Two grades older, the new rich kid from North Little Rock. Shoulda figured it'd be a rich kid.

His soul was smoldering in flames of hate. His hands fisted at his sides.

Toby glanced over, seemingly shocked. Then his face relaxed. "Oh. You." He scoffed. "What are *you* looking at, redneck?"

Mary gasped. Locked eyes with him. "Timmy. I didn't realize. I mean I didn't . . . " Her hand rose to her lips.

He started toward them, teeth gritted.

"Bend over!"

He jumped with a start. Glanced left.

Bent to her charge, Gentle Ben jammed accusingly at him, Old Battle Ax steamed forward.

What the . . .

Then he remembered:

"Timmy Loveless. Bathroom duty. Scrub it good, all the way down the bowl. Before recess! I see one spot o' piss in there, I put the board to you. And don't leave it wet, or I put the board to you. And don't you

*dare go runnin' for that playground before it's done,
or I put the board to you!* You hear me boy?"

Not here.

Not now.

Hair ensnared in the woman's fist, bent cruelly
over her knee, he was pinned facing the oak.

Toby's sneer was a punch in the gut.

Mary wept, but her tears only mocked him.

Grimacing on every blow, his eyes burned holes in
the rich kid's face. He snarled under his breath,
"Handle!"

No one heard but Timmy.

— —

Say you don't like my hair?
Say you don't like my face?
Well I don't like the way you live
I think it's a dis-grace!

Tug-o-War.

Droning tires and a strange red glow pushed Jessi
toward delirium, then nightmare images of her mott-
led-skinned mother mired in melted ice cream
dragged her back toward wakefulness. This dark
death-metal, speakers distorted, provided the winning
edge to the latter.

Her cheeks were damp. Sweat and dried tears,
maybe some blood. She wiped her face with her jacket
sleeve.

Her groans disturbed her. Hoarse, raspy, they didn't sound like her.

She smacked her lips. Grimaced. It tasted like a cat had crapped in her mouth as she slept.

And what is with that crazy music?!

Something poking her ribs. Annoying but not too painful yet. She tried to roll away, but discovered she was pinned somehow.

She sighed and let her eyes fall shut, too tired to care.

Glowing amoebas on the backs of her eyelids, and points of light. Lime green ponies and pastel rainbows materialized on a background of black. Her name in pink, flower dot over the *i—Mommy* in blue balloon letters.

The Drawing Wall.

She remembered the day of its creation.

A pristine kitchen wall of white, a Sharpie left at the counter's edge. Four-year-old Jessi could not resist. A few minutes and countless scribbles later, she realized what she'd done. She tried without success to clean it with her hand.

She considered the marker. Maybe hide it? Or maybe if she just lost herself in play, the marks would go away.

Mama rounded the corner. Jessi looked up, owl-eyed. Her chin began to tremble.

But Mama just laughed. "Well, isn't that *beautiful!* What is it, honey? A pony?"

"Wainbow." Jessi smiled, pointed to another scribble. "And dath *M* for *Mama.*'"

"Well now, there is one little problem."

She tensed a little as her mom squatted.

"You see, Sharpies won't erase. So we're stuck with these pictures and won't be able to draw new ones." She brushed a strand of hair back from Jessi's face. "So how about we do a special project today? We'll make this *whole thing* into a chalkboard." Her hand traced an arc at the wall. "You can draw anything you like, then just erase it when you're ready for new pictures. Whatdya say?" She tweaked Jessi's nose.

Jessi loved drawing. She loved mama-daughter projects even more. She nearly knocked her mother over with a hug.

From around the corner, the bedroom door whined open. Mom gasped in surprise—then called over her shoulder, "Hey! Daddy!" She looked back at Jessi and bounced her eyebrows.

Dad shuffled up behind Mom, loosing a yawn, rubbing his face. "What you girls up to?" He smiled and winked down at Jessi. "Makin' trouble, no doubt."

Mom stood and turned to him. They embraced; Dad kissed the top of her head. "Mornin'."

Mama pulled back, still locked in his arms— "Mornin' yourself, crazy hair." —and ironed out his pajama top with her hands. "Hows about you drive up t' Ace's and get us girls some paint?"

"Whatdya give me?"

"Nothin'." Jessi looked back and forth between the grownups. "But I might could arrange somethin' for Big Rocky and the Stoners."

Jessi: "Who's Rocky?"

"Lil' lady like you? Why, you couldn't handle ole Rocky."

("Who's Rocky?")

"Tough talker."

("What's a stoner?")

"Keep on, woman. See what you get."

"Way I remember it—" Mama poked his chest. "—last time it's *you* got his spine whipped outta place."

("Daddy got a whuppin'?")

Dad leaned down and pecked Mom on the lips.

("Who's Rocky?")

He bent to Jessi, snatched her up like a giant ear of corn and munched on her tummy. *("Num num num . . . ")*

Jessi was a wiggle-worm, squealing with delight.

She found herself staring at the red glow. Why had she run off like that? Stupid stupid *stupid!* And why hadn't she screamed right away, the moment she'd realized she was in trouble? Why hadn't she followed *any* of the self-defense rules?

Come to think of it, she *had* followed them. Or at least she'd tried. But nothing had worked. Maybe because the rules were just no good.

The third and most important self-defense rule of all flashed before her, as if in bright red chalk on the Drawing Wall:

NEVER GIVE UP.

Master Pastor had explained this was easier said than done. You could apply it on a football field, or in the ring, but there was no way to really understand what it meant in combat. The most you could do was talk about it, pray about it, and try your best to be prepared.

You may find yourself severely injured. A loved one may be badly hurt or, God forbid, dead.

Jessi's chin quivered.

But if you're still breathing, that means God still has a plan for you. He *wants you to live, so you need to find that desire within yourself. Cry if you have to, but you* survive!

Even as his voice rang in her ears, she gritted her teeth and kicked the back of the taillight. It accomplished nothing, but it felt good.

She did it again—and thought she felt it budge a little. She knitted her brow, intrigued.

The jacket pinned her tight, held her too close to draw a suitable chamber. Despite her efforts, she was unable to pull it free.

She wormed, struggled . . . finally shrugged out of the jacket—

and the music stopped.

Oh God.

Vision thrumming with her pounding pulse, she held her breath.

Five seconds . . .

Ten . . .

I'll be coming back—
WITH A VENGEANCE
(Machine Man!)
I'll be comin' back—
WITH A VENGEANCE
(Machine Man!)

She let out her pent up breath. The disgusting noise she'd wished away was now an old friend home from a long trip.

She scooted into position, braced her hand on the trunk lid, and locked in on the red glow. *Just like breaking a board.* She tucked her knee to her chest, took several quick breaths—then kicked with all her might.

The fixture broke free.

She sat gawking at what she'd done, at the night staring back at her through the breech in the car.

She scrambled to the mounting hole and peered out.

Someone following. Way behind, but *there.*

The taillight must still be attached, dangling by the wiring, for a pulsing puddle of red chased the car, almost directly beneath her.

She stuck her hand out into the night. Searching blindly. Snared the fixture. She began waving it in the darkness. But who would notice it first, the follower or Machine Man? Well, that was a chance she'd just have to take.

This was probably a waste of time at best, digging her hole deeper at worst. But what else could she do?

She kept waving.

＝ ＝

Brownie mix. Fill up the tank. Fifty-fifty shot at which one he chose to do first. Of course he'd chosen poorly.

The van lurched and sputtered on its last dying gasps.

"Damn it!" Devin struck the wheel with his palm. The van surged ahead, teasing him—then died for good. He rocked back and forth, shoving at the wheel as if he could somehow *will* the vehicle forward.

His heart leapt into his throat when he realized the power-steering was dead. He wrenched right, then left, with all his might, careful not to overdo it, trying to keep it in the road.

He lost speed. Rolled to a crawl. Slowed to a halt.

The red-eyed cyclops faded into the night. He kicked open the door and started pushing. What he hoped to accomplish he didn't know.

His arms began to tremble. His thighs grew numb. He finally relented when a spike drove into his ribs.

He reached inside and teased the wheel right, steered to the side of the road.

He jumped back inside, left hand on the open door handle. Twisted the key. The engine turned over but of course didn't catch. He twisted it again, and again and again—until the chuckle of the engine dwindled to grunts, then a muted sigh.

Then only the dimming of the dashboard lights.

Until now, he'd never fully appreciated the power of an internal combustion engine. Without it, the van was a beached whale, a behemoth corpse even now entering the first stages of decomposition.

He told his students, *Never Give Up*. How easy it had been to play Mister Master Know-it-All in the comfort of the pulpit or standing before his class.

His face burned with shame. He'd been shoveling heaping loads of bullshit. Because of course sometimes you *had* to give up.

Like now.

His eyes wandered down the endless highway. In his memory, the gyrating taillight. He shook his head, and a smile stole around his ear. Then a chuckle escaped him. *What a kid.*

He pulled open the door for Jessi ("Why thank you, sir."), then followed her into the lobby. A cavern, it heard their footsteps and replied in triplicate. Spiraling crepe streamers sagged wall to wall, bouncing buoyantly on a breeze unfelt by the living. They seemed to welcome everyone but him.

Hand-in-hand, they approached the reception table. Echoes of Michael Jackson blasted from the court, scatting something about a smooth criminal.

He peered up at a student-made sign of tempera paint and glitter: Love You to the Moon and Back. *Bright colors on black poster-board, it featured countless stars and a moon of foil. A smiling stick man sat in the crescent, hand-in-hand with a smiling stick girl. They seemed happy together, up there on the moon.*

"Welcome to the Daddy Daughter Dance!"

Devin's eyes fell back to earth. A thirty-something woman held out two tickets. He said, "Oh, I'm not her father." He tried a chuckle; checked it.

The woman batted her eyes.

"Her Dad, he was a great man." He nodded a little too vigorously.

The woman forced a smile and raised her eyebrows. Her eyes darted to the next couple in line, then back to him. She cleared her throat. "These are for the raffle drawin'?" She was still holding out the tickets.

"Oh." Devin accepted them. Fumbled them. Dropped them. He stooped to retrieve them. From above him, the woman said, "Welcome to the Daddy Daughter Dance!"

He stood, said, "Sorry," and extracted himself from the line.

Jessi took his hand. "Come on." She led him out onto the dance floor. Spots of light raced toward him, past him, caprice spirits at a game of chase. He glanced up at the mirror ball.

Movement to his left drew his attention. Balloons like ghosts stood vigil over the dance, swaying and bobbing, tethered to earth at each basketball hoop.

He felt eyes upon him. A father embracing his daughter. Devin nodded, then turned away, only to find the eyes of yet another dad. The man smiled politely, then a spin stole his gaze away.

So many daughters, each with a father. A real *father, the man who conceived her, the only man who should ever—*

"A-hem." *Jessi's right arm stood poised like the neck of a swan. So delicate, so vulnerable; he'd never seen it that way before.*

He took her hand and embraced her. James Taylor was crooning, You got a friend. *Devin's eyes continued scanning the dancers. He felt like a shoplifter watching for cops.*

"You don't have to do that, you know."

He looked down at Jessi. "Did I step on your toes?"

"Back at the table. I'm not her father. You don't have to do that."

"But I'm not your father."

"So?" *She laid her head on his chest.*

After a half minute or so, he drew a breath and shook his head. "I just don't want anyone to think I'm trying to replace him."

She looked back up at him. "Anyone, or me?"

Devin shrugged.

"Well are you?"

"Am I what?"

"Trying to replace him?"

He opened his mouth to speak, then snapped it shut.

"Gotcha."

"Why am I not surprised?" *He managed an awkward smile.*

"Look. No one can replace anyone else. But they can *fill* a position. Daddy had an important one.

You're not replacing him, just taking over his duties, that's all."

Devin nodded.

"And doing a bang-up job of it, if you ask me." She laid her head back on his chest.

His eyes clouded. He squeezed them shut, then took a calming breath. "Who are you, anyway? Rasputin in a ponytail?"

She looked up at him, from one of his eyes to the other, then creased her brow. "I'm a survivor." There was no escaping her gaze. "You are, too." After a beat, she nodded. "Now. Let's try and survive this dance."

Bullshit or not, Jessi had listened to his sermons—and *believed*.

And she hadn't given up.

He shoved open the van door. Stepped out and slammed it shut. He started walking—now jogging—ribs on fire, gazing wide-eyed down the highway at his brilliant bursts of pain.

━ ━

The headlights faded, shrinking as the distance steadily increased—then disappeared altogether.

Flat tire? Piss break?

Hell, who cares? "Happy trails, fuck stick." Loveless leaned back into the headrest and took a trip home.

3:00 p.m. Thanksgiving Day, 7th grade:
Timmy pushed through the can-lid door in camo
pants and KISS t-shirt. A cold breath of wind arrived
in his wake, and a slash of sunlight. "Mama, what are
we havin'—"

"Tryin' to melt the snow?" Gus Loveless sat in
gloom. Sprawled in a dilapidated Lazy Boy. Dirty
frayed plaster encased one foot, all the way up to his
knee. Five toes like bloated boils peeked out. Swollen
to the bursting point. A little louder, he said, "You
bleedin' us, boy." A smoldering Marlboro failed to
mask the stink of lard cooked into the walls.

Daddy *always* seemed to be wearing a cast. Or an
eye patch. Or covered in stitches or toting a crutch.
His mane was shorn from a rabid wolf's tail and
framed his face in strands. *"Boy!"* The TV colored him
electric blue—then red then gold then shades of yellow. "Shut the damn door, dumbass!"

An audience of manikins roared in laughter, seemingly at Timmy. Daddy turned pale orange, flashed
instantly green in the haze.

Timmy turned and closed the door, then padded to
the kitchen. "What's for supper tonight?" He dropped
into a chair at the Formica-topped table. A 40-watt
bug-bulb cast yellow shadows on the floor.

Mama was watching the microwave, her face distorted in the back-splash of light. Curlers made val-
iant attempts at escape. A nightgown like a threadbare
shroud did not entirely conceal the mummy within.
"Comin' right up." Her first two fingers stood erect,

clamping a Virginia Slim. A thread of smoke curled from the tip and became one with a putrid cloud.

Ding!

She popped the door and reached inside.

Snatched her hand back. "God*damn* it!" She cooled the burn on a luke-warm Budweiser. Took a swig while she was at it.

"I meant Thanksgivin' dinner."

"What y' think this is?" The plastic platter plopped to the table. She peeled off the cover and tossed it to the sink where it capped a mountain of dishes. She downed the beer, tossed the can, and rounded the table. Headed for the back.

Timmy stared down at the sectioned tray: A slab of worn shoe-leather drowned in snot. A triangle of pale puss laced in yellow. Rubber cubes of neon hues, much brighter than anything grown in the ground. All steaming like a warm pile left at a fire hydrant. "This ain't turkey!"

Mama stopped. Turned. She shot her hip and planted her fist on it.

"I'm talkin' about *real* turkey. And dressing."

"My cookin' ain't good enough for you?"

"With cranberry sauce."

She glanced at the TV, back to Timmy. Smirked and batted her eyes.

"A *night*-time supper."

She sucked on her cigarette. "Well, I'm *workin'* tonight!"

"On Thanksgiving?"

She yelled toward the den. "Well somebody around here's gotta brang in some damn money!" A blast of blue smoke punctuated each plosive.

From the den: "I'm all busted up here, bitch! I *cain't* work!"

("Maybe candles? And pumpkin pie?")

"Well whose fault is that, Lightin' McQueen?"

("You know, a feast.")

Mama turned to Timmy, Gus forgotten. Smoke still wafted through gaps in her teeth. "A feast, you say." She chuckled, incredulous.

Timmy shrugged.

Her eyes narrowed. "Look like you eatin' plenty to me." She sucked another drag, hollowing her face. She never blew smoke out but *talked* it out, her words seemingly smoldering. "T' hell's wrong with you anyway? All swole up with bulges like you got the cantcer."

"Mama, please. I only meant—"

"That's just *weird*. Ain't but twelve and got more muscles than your daddy." She raised her voice and yelled at the den. *"Not that that's sayin' much!"*

("Bitch, I am keepin' a runnin' damn tally and you are gonna pay for *ever' word!"*)

"It's *you* gettin' the cancer!" Timmy's breath kicked up. "Your hair's fallin' out from all your smokin' and drinkin'!"

I only drink Mountain Dew and Budweiser. Her maxim, her motto. *Fish piss in water. Makes me sick just thankin' about it.* She was a skeleton, feisty as a snake.

She took another puff of venom. "My hair." She scoffed. *"My* hair?" Her eyes bit into him. "Least I got girl's hair. Problem is, *you do too!"*

("You gone cut that mop, boy.")

"Yeah? Well what about yores, white-trash Sampson?" Her shouting triggered a coughing spasm. Beet-faced and bent, it seemed she'd hack up a liver.

("Mother fucker, I will crawl over there and break this cast off in your ass!")

Eyes puffed from the exertion, she said to Timmy, "I got news for you." She jabbed two brown-stained fingers at him— "Boys ain't supposed to have girl faces." —cigarette smoldering between. "Look at them lips." She took another puff as if making her point. "All puffed up like they got stung by bees or something. Look like one them queer Calvin Clean models standin' around in his damn underpants." Someone on the TV shouted, *Score!* A mob of fans erupted with cheers.

Timmy pushed back from the table. "Nuh uh!"

"Awww. Poor baby. Gone cry now? Gone run tell?"

Timmy shot to his feet, hands fisted at his sides. *"Stop* it!" The chair behind him clattered to the floor.

("Tryin' to watch TV in here.")

"Got a skirt hid up that ass?" She snuffed the butt in her uneaten mush. "Sissy." It looked like roadkill, a single ear inexplicably intact, jutting from the sludge.

"I *hate* you!"

She snarled in rage, each eye a flamethrower. She shot forward. In one quick motion, she snared Timmy's platter and mashed it in his face.

The hands of every clock stood still; he floated in outer space.

(Raucous laughter.)

Buzzing in his ears, warm snot oozing down his face—

(Hacking, coughing, out of control.)

—and caked heavy like mud on his shirt.

("Oh my God!" More raucous laughter.)

He spit out a chunk of something, loath to lick it.

Mama materialized, slapping her knee— *"Lil' Timmy shit-face!"* —and jabbing her finger at him. *"Lil' Timmy shit face!"* Husking out guffaws.

He gasped for breath. Couldn't seem to feel his hands.

"Lil' Timmy Shit-Face! Lil' Timmy Shit-Face!"

("I'm tryin' to watch Goddamn TEE-vee!")

Late that night: *The air was sweet and heavy as corn syrup.*

Her ponytail poured from a smelter's cauldron, bounced in waves as she floated through a field of marigolds.

She slowly turned to him, walking backwards now. Floating. Bees and tiny butterflies flitted, garnished her halo of sunlight.

Mary held her arms out to him. "I got your feast."

He cocked his head.

"Even brought you punkin' pie."

He tried in vane to close the distance. She faded even faster.

"Just like you wanted."

Timmy's eyes popped open.

Mama sat in shadows, beside him on the bed. A cigarette dangled from her lips. When she sucked a puff, her face glowed orange in the strange luminance. She squinted at him through the smoke. "Sit on up and have a bite." She patted a stack of pillows piled behind him.

He scooted into position. "You was mean to me." A golden glint from her breast caught his eye: *Waffle House* in blocks of yellow, *Robin* in black type underneath.

"Aw now, don't you pay me no mind when I git like that." Her eyes were puffed and veined in red, like she'd just trod through a forest fire. "People say stuff they don't mean when they're drunk." She set a Styrofoam box in his lap, *Thank You* embossed on the lid.

He smiled up at her.

Mama smiled back. "Close your eyes."

"Huh?"

"Go on, close 'em now."

Blind now in the gloom, he heard the bedsprings complain, like she was reaching for something. "Keep 'em closed." Her lighter whisked. Through sealed eyelids, a yellow blossom bloomed. "A'right, open!"

A slice of pumpkin pie; a wad of melting Cool Whip. A candle askew in the goo. The tiny fire warmed his heart.

He smiled up at her again. "Thanks, Mama."

"There's turkey 'n dressing in the fridge, too. I figured you'd wanna get right to dessert." She plucked up the plastic fork, forked a wedge of sugar and spice.

"Wanna know what I really think?" She lifted it to his mouth. "You the handsomeist boy in all Arkansas."

They sat in silence as she nursed his wounds, feeding him pumpkin pie.

When he finished, she set the box aside. Looked into his eyes. After a time, she said, "Your hair is like a lion's mane." She stroked it in the darkness. "Beautiful." Gently bunched it in her fist, lightly shook his head. *"Powerful."*

Her hand slid down; her fingertips tickled his forehead. Pleasant chills spilled down his neck and trickled into his spine.

"And your face?" Roaming, seemingly lost— "It b'longs on a Roman coin." —her fingers traced his eyebrows. "I see you—" Tickled his neck. "—standin' atop a big ole hill." Massaged his shoulder. "Dark clouds in the distance." Stroked his chest as if finger-painting. "That lion's mane just a blowin' in the breeze."

From outside, a chorus of crickets lulled him.

Her curled pointer slipped under his chin. She lifted it, ever so slightly. She caressed his lips with her thumb, at first tenderly, then more insistently.

Of its own accord, his jaw relaxed.

She penetrated his mouth. Traced his lower teeth. When she pushed inside, he suckled her thumb, relished every loop and whorl. It tasted salty. Buttery.

Mama smiled.

She leaned forward, lids drooping, eyes swimming. Her gaze dropped to his lips. The thumb slid out, his chin still propped on her pointer. She held him there, swaying gently as if by a breeze felt only by her. Eyes locked on his lips. He did not resist.

She swiped the corner of his mouth with her thumb.

After a beat, she sat back up and sucked away a smudge of Cool Whip. "You got it bad for that Mary."

Timmy blushed and looked at his hands.

"I understand, I really do. She's a pretty lil' ole thing. You been knowin' her since grade school and can't hardly get her out your mind."

He looked back up at her.

"Baby, what you got to realize is, that girl is *changed*. Ain't no good no more, eyes on that ole book school."

He blinked.

"Oh I see her. Way she dresses like she somebody special? Got her nose stuck up them rich kids' asses?"

He didn't know what to think, what to say.

"That girl is puttin' on *airs!*"

He shifted positions, though he wasn't uncomfortable.

"Rich folks, they care about nobody."

He looked at his hands again.

"I know what happened to Toby Thompson."

His eyes darted back to mama. The trailer creaked at a gust of wind; something howled in the distance.

"You do too, don't you?"

He tried to swallow, couldn't. It seemed he was nodding, but he couldn't be certain.

"They can drag that river all they want. Run them dogs 'til their sniffers fall off."

Screams in his mind, and begging and pleading. Punctuated with thuds.

"Won't never find him—"

A can of gasoline.

"—will they?"

A mound of ashes, out behind the dump.

"Not around these parts anyway."

He creased his brow.

"If they find him at all, it'll be out west. Maybe all the way to California. Dead, more'n likely." She shrugged. "Or locked in some pervert's basement."

Timmy released a breath he hadn't realized he'd held.

"Thinks he can make it on his own. Don't give a shit about what he might be doing to his family."

Timmy nodded. Maybe too much?

Her eyes clouded with concern. "That's Mary now, honey." She stroked his face. "Don't care about family, don't care about you. Don't care about nobody but herself." Her hand dropped back to the bed. "She's gone, honey. Ain't never comin' back." After a beat, she smiled. "But I'll let y' in on a little a secret."

"Yeah?"

She propped on one arm. "This ole world's full o' girls."

He creased his brow again.

"Oh yes it is." She flashed her Mama crocodile grin, wise as Yoda, sly as a fox. "See, they's *lots* o' Marys, Timmy. Lots of better ones. Not like this stuck-up Mary. You got to let this one go, so you can keep a eye peeled for *yore* Mary." Her eyes wandered to the window. "One day you gonna turn around, and there she'll be." She smiled up at the ceiling. "In all her glory." She looked back at him. *"Your* Mary. True heart, humble mind, and finer n' a frog hair."

He looked at his hands, then back up at mama. "Sing me a lullaby?"

She looked at him for a half a minute, maybe more. As she stared, a cloud formed in her eyes. "I don't remember none, baby." She slowly shook her head.

He sighed, eased down into the covers and curled himself away from her. Eyes still open.

Minutes passed. Was she still there? Maybe he'd dozed without realizing it. Maybe she'd gone as he slept.

"If I say, to you, tomorrow." A Capella, but a silent singing guitar accompanied her.

"Take my hand child, come with me."

Strumming his pain.

"It's to a castle, I will take you."

He rolled back around to face her.

"Where what's to be, they say, will be."

The hour was late. Even the crickets, it seemed, had turned in for the night.

"Is that a lullaby?"

"It's Led Zeppelin, honey."

"Know any more?"

She smiled down at him and raised her eyebrows. "And if you say, to me, tomorrow."

He lost himself in her eyes.

"Oh what fun, it all, would be."

Her voice tried to soar, but the weight of a fallen moon seemed to pin her to earth. "Then what's to stop us, pretty baby."

She bent, kissed his forehead. His eyes fell shut.

"But what is—and what should never be."

— —

Revelations 6:7-8

And when he had opened the fourth seal, I heard the voice of the fourth beast say, *Come and see.*

And I looked, and behold a pale horse: and his name that sat on him was Death, and Hell followed with him. And power was given unto them over the fourth part of the earth, to kill with sword, and with hunger, and with death, and with the beasts of the earth.

— —

Well shit. It was open. Now why the hell didn't they just close at sundown like every other damn country store? Trying to be like 7-11, he guessed. He'd have rather done this without a fuss, but this is what he had. He wanted—*needed*—to talk with his Lil' Mary, needed to know *now.*

He couldn't just stop on the side of the road. Sure as shit, some do-gooder—maybe even Johnny Law—would come rolling up to see was he broke down. That wouldn't be no good for nobody. He just wanted some peace and quiet, needed some damn privacy.

Well, too bad for whoever was working tonight.

Tim Loveless pulled the Buick into the Toot-n-Moo bait shop, grocery store, and service station (Paul & Ruth Davis, proprietors). Some old lady sat alone at the counter, thumbing through a magazine. She glanced up as he parked at the pumps, then went right back to reading. Didn't pay him no mind. Not that it mattered.

The parking lot was empty, the road deserted. *Well alright then.*

He removed his D-shades, raincoat, and shoulder holster rig. He jammed the .45 into his waistband. He shrugged into a flannel shirt and buttoned it up. He left it untucked to conceal the weapon.

He bounced from the car, a jolly spring in his step, whistling a country tune. His size was intimidating, so he'd long since learned to play it friendly-like when he needed to. He headed straight for the side of the building to the men's room, gazing out at the highway as he strolled, just another hayseed with his head up his ass.

The door squeaked open on rusty hinges.

Dropping the dumb-shit act, he headed over to the sink. He wanted everything to be just so. He'd thought he found her countless times before. Blonds, of course, but also brunettes and red heads, curly hair and straight. She ought to be blond, but you just never could tell.

Wrong, wrong, wrong. Ever' single one. They was all Marys, but none of them was *his* Mary.

This one was different. He just had a feeling, oh yes he did.

He bent to check his face in the mirror.

Shit. His feisty little angel done a good job on his ole nose, and his hair looked like it come off a damn wet dog. Smelled like one, too.

He rinsed the blood off his face. Sucked water up his nose, blew it in the sink. Threw a splash in his hair and combed his fingers through it. That seemed to kill the smell pretty good. He cranked out a wad of paper towels and dried his hands and face.

He re-examined the mirror, turning his head side to side. "You handsome devil." He winked at himself, then turned for the door.

━ ━

Headlights.

Most people in Arkansas would stop to assist a stranded motorist, even pick up a hitchhiker. At least they used to. But the effects of an ever-increasing crime rate had wormed their way into rural America, if not by violence itself then by reports of violence in the outside world. Of course, after tonight, nothing would ever be the same.

Devin had been thinking about this moment as he jogged down the highway. It seemed boldness would be the best way to play it, a desperate gesture rather than just thumbing it from the side of the road. So as the headlights approached, he moved to the center stripes and began waiving his arms. He heard the craft before he could see it—a deep hum as if from a nuclear-powered engine, metal-on-metal buzzing, sibilant electric counter-rhythm battling the thrum at triple speed. His heart seemed to synchronize with the noise.

Closer now, it took on new strangeness. He slowly lowered his arms and creased his brow. Rather than bright white, the headlights were a spectral luminance, a constantly shifting non-color. The vessel seemed to float on a blanket of blue light, as if not of this world.

Devin squinted, shielded his eyes and braced himself.

━ ━

The red beacon brightened in her hand, then dimmed. Bright-dim-bright-dim . . . and the pitch of the tire-drone descended.

Jessi dropped the taillight as if it were scalding. Hauled in her arm and shoved herself back. Wide-eyed, she stared at the blinking ambient glow.

She shot forward and jammed her arm back out. Fumbled for the light. Vertigo dizzied her as the car veered left, straightened, then veered right. She grasped the cord, reeled in the fixture. Tried without success to fix it back in place.

They slowed to a halt. The music ceased but the engine still rumbled. She kept fumbling. Ten seconds passed. Fifteen. Still no luck with the light. The faint stink of exhaust began to worry her. *What is he doing up there?* "Come on, come on . . . " The taillight refused to cooperate.

The engine died, and the red light. Jessi held her breath. Pulse pounding. She kept tension on the cord, hoping the taillight would appear normal from outside.

The driver's door opened. After a beat, it banged shut, rocking the car.

She gritted her teeth, listening for the tell-tale jingle, the rattle of a key in the trunk.

He started whistling as if everything was fine and dandy.

Huh?

The tune faded away.

She gently payed out the cord until it assumed the fixture's weight—then set to work shoving on the lid. Of course it wouldn't budge.

She searched blindly for the trunk latch, feeling her way in the dark. Maybe she could somehow unlock it from the inside. Or maybe—

What's this?

In the killer's haste to dump her in the trunk and clean up his mess, he'd slammed the lid on the tail of her jacket. Right at the latch.

"Oh please, God." She spun quickly onto her back and tucked her knees to her chest. The trunk was roomy but not enough so for a good chamber. But if the latch wasn't fully engaged due to the obstructing jacket . . .

She pushed as best she could, making the most of her cramped quarters.

The lid held firm.

She whipped over onto all fours and threw the back of her elbow into the unmoving plate of steel.

Her bony arm would more likely dent the lid than move it, only to leave her elbow black and blue.

"It's okay, Jess. Don't give up, don't give up." She fought back hysteria.

She laid on her left side, feet facing backward. Instead of kicking *up*, she aimed for the union of the top and back of the lid. Her hope was that the kick would apply force both up *and* out, freeing the latch and popping the trunk.

Slam!

Nothing.

Again and again, she really laid into it. It seemed she might be making some progress . . .

The trunk lid yawned open and bounced on its hinges.

She squinted at the brilliance of a gas-pump island, half expecting the monster to pop up from behind the car, silhouetted like a haunted-house prop.

The island remained deserted.

She scrambled from the trunk, grabbed her jacket, and sprinted for the market.

An antique school bell chimed above her as she shoved through the door.

The store was warm and dry, lined with an unfinished plank floor under a gabled ceiling. Fishing tackle, camping supplies, canned food and other items stood lined like soldiers on wooden shelves. Several ceiling fans turned gently. The gurgle of a minnow tank and chirp of bait crickets lulled her.

A woman in her fifties sat on a stool behind the counter, looking up from a tabloid. Her beryl blue eyes promised mischief, seemed to have rejected the years that aged the rest of her. "Well hello there, sprout. Welcome to the Toot-n-Moo."

Jessi stood transfixed, not believing her luck. She blinked to make sure she wasn't dreaming.

"Ruth Davis, proprietor. Lemme know can I help you find somethin'." Her smile proved to be a match for her eyes.

Jessi glanced around the shop. "Where is he?"

"Where's who? Your daddy?"

He wasn't here. Wasn't here *now*.

She bolted for the checkout counter. Pushed through the swinging half-door to Ruth's side. "Call 911." Not a whisper but under her breath.

The lady just creased her brow.

Louder now: "Didn't you hear me? Call the police!"

"Now just calm down a minute, sweet pea." She leaned over and placed a calming hand on Jessi's shoulder. "Don't do no good gettin' worked up, no sir. 'Cause the Lord don't never put more on ye than you can handle." She winked. "Now. Just take a deeeep breath and tell me what's the problem. You lose your mom and daddy?"

Why didn't grownups ever *listen?* She was going to have to spell it out. "Look. We were at Piggly Wiggly getting school thupplies." She cringed. *Forget the lisp!* "Me n' Mom. Master Pastor was there. It started raining, and I should have waited, but I ran outside. When I got to the car—"

Jessi gasped at the tinkle of the school bell.

"Why lookie here. I bet this is your Daddy coming now."

She dropped. Tucked her knees tightly to her tummy.

Ruth cleared her throat and brushed at her hair. "He's a tall drink o' water, ain't he?" Aside, eyes glued to the front.

Jessi pressed her back to the shelves under the checkout counter. She shook her head and gestured desperately at the woman.

"Evenin', handsome." Ruth didn't seem to know what to do with her hands. "Welcome to the Toot-n-Moo. Now, did you happen to lose your little—"

"Key to the men's room?" Voice as if from a fifty-gallon drum.

"Aw, it ain't locked." Ruth batted her eyes and smiled.

"Yeah, I know. I been in there already." A chuckle as if from the Jolly Green Giant. "I'm just fuckin' with you."

The woman's smile faded. She shot a subtle glance down and to her left, almost looked right at her. Jessi prayed Machine Man had missed it. She hunkered tighter still, became one with the shelves.

What's he doing? Why is she just sitting there?

Ruth's face sagged. She began to tremble. "Please, mister." Her hand crept from her side, seemingly feeling for Jessi's shoulder.

The blast shook the windows. Ruth *flew* off the stool as if she'd been kicked. Slammed against the wall. She slid to the floor, plopped onto her butt.

Hands draped at her sides. Legs parted. Smear of gore down the wall.

Her head tilted impossibly sideways, as if to make room for the scarlet geyser. She sat staring at Jessi, expressionless.

The geyser died to rhythmic pulses. Ruth gagged and fidgeted, heels tapping. She slowly lifted her left arm, fingers relaxed, like the ghost from *A Christmas Carol*. Seemingly reaching for Jessi. Still expressionless. Rivulets of blood ran down her arm and dripped onto her lap.

The arm thumped to the floor like a dead fish. She gurgled; a final eruption oozed down her breast—and her crystal blue eyes fixed on the world beyond.

Jessi realized she'd clamped her hand over her mouth. She'd yelped like a kicked dog when the gun went off. She was certain of it. But had it even passed her lips? If so, had it been swallowed by the report?

A hand like a fat steak reached around the counter and snared a set of keys from a hook. He jerked the phone off the wall. After a beat, a crash startled her, followed by an avalanche of canned goods.

Boot steps clumped along the wooden floor. She riveted her eyes to the swinging half-door, waiting for him to push through.

Clump, clump . . .

She held her breath.

Clump. Clump, clump.

With a subtle click, she found herself sitting in gloom, bathed in the ambient glow of the pump-island fluorescents.

More boot steps. The school-bell tinkled. The door fell closed; the lock rattled. *Thank you, God. Oh thank you, Jesus.*

She huddled in the sickly light, crickets chirping, minnow water gurgling. She pulled in her feet, doing her best to avoid the dark pool expanding to a lake on the floor.

━ ━

Tim Loveless locked the doors behind him, smiling at the memory of that bitch's face when he'd been fucking with her—then when he'd blown her damn head off.

He headed toward the car. After but three steps, his pace slowed. He realized he didn't know how to start this, didn't know what to *say*. Would Little Mary be scared when she didn't recognize where she was at? Surely not. Surely she'd feel safe with a big ole man like Tim Loveless here to protect her.

He decided he'd just first thing let her know he'd always watch out for her, always do right by her, always be there to—

What. Tha. Fuck.

The driver's side taillight hung from its wiring. Worse, the trunk lid stood slightly ajar.

He did a quick scan of his memory, wondering if maybe he'd opened it.

Hell no.

He lurched forward, lifted the lid.

Empty. No damn surprise.

He creased his brow and scanned the compartment anyway, unbelieving.

Flummoxed, he turned to the glistening highway.

He took off as if by a starting gun.

After five steps, he stumbled to a halt.

The old bitch had started to say something, hadn't she? Oh yes she had. What was it? And had she glanced down? If so, what had she glanced *at?*

He turned on his heel and bolted back to the Toot-n-Moo.

Chapter 3

The voice again. Familiar somehow. Why won't she show herself? Where does she go when she isn't here? Why can't she seem to hear me?

I dreamed of her. In the dream, her face. She is a friend. Closer than a friend. We laughed and played, out in the sunshine, the blessed light.

The thing rose from the mud, perhaps formed itself from it. Worms oozed from its flesh. A beetle skittered down its eyeless face.

We fled, ran until I couldn't feel the legs beneath me. For all the good it did.

It moves outside the laws of physics. Hide and it will find you. A tree with groping branches. Swollen vine like a spiny squid tentacle. A hole in the earth, slick with mud, lined with stone teeth.

Turn and there it is, teeth bared, baboon face, savage barking . . . blood, gore, limb from limb, severed heads—all dead, all dead.

Only the two of us survive.

She stands between the beast and me, small but brave, weak but willing. It approaches, taunting us. Closer . . . snarling . . .

I bolt awake in soaking sheets, choking off a scream. The dream dissipates, and her face, scattered like ashes to the wind.

Did it hear my silent scream? Has it crawled from the abyss? Slinking toward me in the dark?

Closer now?

Closer . . . Closer . . .

— —

As the vessel approached, the barrel-deep voice of what was apparently a very pissed off black man cut through the noise, oozing vulgarities to the brain-rattling beat of gansta rap.

Devin thought he recognized the car, what the kids called a low-rider. The Whitlock brothers, from what he could tell. Probably on their way back from Little Rock. Not what he'd been expecting, but this is what he had.

The Whitlock boys were examples of a strangely common phenomenon in predominately white backwoods boroughs. Like any adolescents, kids from these towns sought independence. Their own way of doing things, their own music. Their parents listened to country, and rock-n-roll had grown pathetically impotent with the introduction of bands featuring lipstick-wearing, emaciated boys pouting about getting their hearts broken by psychologically abusive women. Rap offered a tough alternative. Sadly, with the music came a culture of violence, racism, and an utter disrespect for women.

As the car neared, Devin's teeth began to rattle in sync with the beat. It slowed—then finally stopped not five feet in front of him.

"Jimmy! Johnny!"

They just sat there, engine idling, hosing him down with the headlights.

Devin shaded his eyes. "Turn it down a minute!"

The engine screamed and the car lurched forward. Devin skipped/scooted back, barely avoiding the bumper as the Toyota barked to a stop.

It lurched again.

This time, hands on the hood, he vaulted to the driver's side. He waited, heart pounding.

Was that raucous laughter under the music? What if he'd been mistaken about the owner of the vehicle? Of course, the likelihood of there being more than one car custom-painted half fire and half ice were slim to none. Still, the tinted windows prevented him from being certain. So he stood there like an idiot, looking up and down the deserted highway. Jessi's clock ticking.

He looked back down at the car. The driver's side door exclaimed in airbrush, *2 Cold 2 Hold.*

The music, if you could call it that, diminished to a dull roar. Both doors opened. Jimmy Whitlock, the driver and older of the two, stepped out of the hotrod. His fat gold rings clinked on the door. A ball cap was jammed tight on his head, turned about thirty degrees sideways. Devin had always imagined the bills of these gansta lids to be dials indicating the wearer's level of stupidity.

Jimmy chuckled. "You see dis dumb mutha fucka main? Mutha fucka standin' in the middle da roat, main."

Johnny, the passenger, shook his head and laughed at the pavement, arms propped on the passenger door and roof. A wisp of tightly-trimmed peach fuzz snaked down each jawline, destination a tart goatee that gave the impression he'd just finished sucking a sow. Both boys wore bejeweled gold shades.

Jimmy scowled. "Word up, Preach?" His pants hung around his upper thighs, revealing silk boxers.

Devin suspected that not even black gansta-rappers spoke with such a thick (headed) accent. But if these guys had been any whiter they'd have been clear. So they over-compensated in order to *become* black, or what they imagined was black. This whole phenomenon grated on Devin's nerves. Why couldn't people just be who they were? "Guys. Please. I need to use your phone."

Jimmy just bobbed his head to the beat.

"We need to call 9-1-1. There's been a—"

"What?" Then to his brother, "Nigga talkin' about calling the po-po n' shit."

Po-po was hillbilly speak. Not gansta. Devin knew that much. Apparently, they'd missed that page in the meat-head manual.

Johnny answered from the passenger's side. "Sheee-it. Mutha fucka *crazy,* main." He began strolling around to the front of the car.

Devin had known these boys from church since they were toddlers. As they'd grown into teens, their attendance had decreased—then ceased altogether a few years ago. Rumor had it they were mixed up with gangs in Little Rock, probably earning their street cred by providing weed grown somewhere in the Arkansas hills. That thought troubled Devin.

More troubling, however, was the stroller incident. About a year ago at the Conway Best Buy, Devin had bumped into Jimmy.

Literally.

The kid had been pushing a baby stroller, of all things, a bus-sized contraption with a sun shade like a pterodactyl wing. Their eyes had met and, judging by the *Don't-Say-a-Goddamn-Word* look he'd received, Devin supposed Jimmy had gotten stuck babysitting. Or maybe he'd gotten some girl pregnant—in which case, hey, hooray for him taking some paternal responsibility.

Later, rounding an isle, Devin had gasped when he ran his shopping cart right into the stroller, spilling the contents onto the terrazzo floor. As it turned out, the carriage had been filled not with diaper donning darlings, but with a load of random store items apparently selected with an eye for both value and compactness.

As Jimmy had assumed the position a few minutes later, they'd locked eyes again. He received loud and clear the boy's silent smoldering promise.

He saw the Whitlocks around town occasionally. Jimmy's spiteful look was always there: *Just you wait, preacher.*

Devin's offers of apology and even free counsel were met with only scowls. What more could he do? In order to change, people had to want to change.

These boys had made up their minds who they wanted to be.

And now here they were.

Great. Just great. Thanks for this, Lord.

Should he offer yet another apology? Of course, bringing it up may serve only to reopen old wounds. With luck, perhaps they'd written it off. Maybe everything was cool. "Look. Guys. There's been a murder and kidna—"

"Still do dat hai-ya shit?" Jimmy again.

"HoooOOO . . . OOOoooooOOO . . . " Johnny's high-pitched Bruce Lee whine came from behind Devin. He imagined the boy's hat was set at about dumb-ass, dumb-ass-and-a-half.

Devin snapped before he realized it. "Godddamn it, would you guys drop the dumb-shit act? Jessi Owen has been—"

The switchblade flicked in his face, utterly unexpected. These guys were way farther down the rat hole than he'd allowed himself to believe, and that had left him vulnerable.

—— ——

Besides forgetting to at least stage the bashed out taillight, she'd left the trunk open. She silently cursed herself for those oversights. Of course, she'd been in kind of a real big hurry, escaping a psychopathic robot and all.

Jessi glanced around the checkout stand for an exit. No door. Only display windows, fixed in place.

Try the back?

No. She'd have to expose herself to the front door, through which Machine Man was probably peering even now.

Her pulse kicked up. Bats in her stomach.

She looked to Ruth. As if she could be of any help. The corpse stared back—not quite at her, but over her left shoulder, the same place she'd glanced when . . .

She followed the blind gaze to the shelves behind her.

Cleaning products.

A folded towel.

Eight-pack of toilet paper.

A purse.

She scrutinized the towel. It had a little bulge to it, didn't it? Bigger than could be explained by a wrinkle in the fold.

She turned and stood. Snatched up the towel.

She gasped. Her eyes widened and her breath kicked up.

The towel dropped to the floor. She reached slowly out to what lay exposed on the shelf. Her hand hovered there, fingers trembling.

She touched it. Snatched her hand back.

She touched it again. Stroked it. But she couldn't bring herself to pick it up.

A sawed-off double-barrel shotgun.

Somewhat rusted, the stock hacked to a duct-tape-wrapped nub—but a *gun*.

In the process of earning her black belt, Master Pastor had required her to learn about firearms. Although she'd fired both pistols and rifles, he'd stressed how she should never try to use one in defense. Not until she was older.

She was not even to so much as touch one. Instead, he'd insisted, *Whenever you see a gun,* run!

Retreat was not an option here. Surely for this pickle, Master Pastor would grant an exception.

But she had two problems. First, she'd been advised shotguns were a whole new ballgame. And this particular contraption looked like it would blow up in her hands.

Second, and most important, her targets had been only pie-plates and tin-cans.

Could she shoot a man? She'd witnessed two murders tonight, one of them her mother's. Would that experience shore up or restrain her resolve? Could she inflict on another human being—even Machine Man— the atrocities she'd seen inflicted on them? She was ten, not six. She realized killing someone would change her life forever—not that she wouldn't be totally Fruit Loops after tonight anyway.

Her chest heaved. Her hands shook. The gun shimmered like a forbidden oasis.

Keys rattling in the door. Then that cursed bell.

She snatched up the shotgun, heavy in her hands, and cocked both hammers.

— —

Tim Loveless scanned the store. There was a chance she took off running down the highway, but he didn't think so. "Come on out, now." His voice resonated in the empty market, deep and strong.

Reassuring.

He crept to the first aisle. "I ain't gonna hurt you none."

Empty.

He realized the Colt was in his hand. He must've drawed it out of sheer instinct outside. He eased it back in his waistband as he peeked around the second aisle. "I just wanna talk to you is all."

No Lil' Mary, as expected.

He tip-toed two paces to the third aisle. "I just figured we ought to get acquainted." Only oil and antifreeze and packs of them dangling Christmas tree car-deodorizers.

Last aisle. "You know, so we can be friends."

Nothing.

He squatted and peered beneath the minnow-tank table just to be sure.

He stood. Turned to the checkout stand. "Are you playin' hide-n-go-seek with me, little girl?" He chuckled. "Why, that sounds like fun."

He took a cat-step toward the counter. "Ready or not, here I come." The gurgle of the minnow tank somewhat masked his footfalls.

He took another silent step. "Oh little Maaaaryyyy." Indeed this *was* fun. A pleasant little shudder ran up his spine. "I know where you're aaaaa—aaat."

And he did. The more he thought about it, it just made sense. She'd somehow busted out the trunk, then run to the nearest hidey-hole she could find: In here with the grandma.

He glanced down when a floor-plank complained—then smiled back up at the checkout counter. "I'm sorry about the old lady, but whose fault is that?"

He tip-toed another step. Almost there. "That's what happens when you misbehave."

Yes, just before he popped the granny, she'd glanced down, hadn't she? Oh yes she had; he was sure of it now. "Little Maaaaa-ryyyy."

He burst through the swinging half-doors. Arms spread, he braced himself, ready to catch the little rabbit when she tried to run past him.

There she stood, just like he expected. His precious little angel. Only instead of being blinded by a holy heavenly halo, he found himself staring down two barrels of a sawed-off shotgun.

— —

Some master you are, pastor. He should have seen this coming, should have expected this from these two.

"Who you callin' dumb-shit, man?" Jimmy scowled, jabbed the blade on *dumb*. The accent was gone. Now he was just a pissed off redneck.

Devin opened his mouth to speak—but froze at the *shoo-clack* of a pistol behind him.

Johnny said, "You a long way from Kansas, Daisy."

Dukes of Hazard or Wizard of Oz. Pick one, dumbass.

"You know how much you cost me, preacher?" Jimmy's words *oozed* out, slow and syrupy, like a backwoods porch-sitter at the bottom of a bottle.

Devin slowly raised his hands, shook his head once.

"Twenty grand."

Johnny echoed from behind Devin, "Twenty grand, boy." He pronounced *boy* like *boink* sans the *nk*. For some reason, this was like nails on a chalkboard to Devin.

"That ain't including the cost of me having a record now."

Devin's raised hands were a gesture of submission, and would hopefully set them at ease. That was a good thing—

("Record, *boi*.")

—because raising his hands also put him in optimal position to address the blade. Of course, the best way to prevent getting your ass kicked—or stabbed or shot—was to avoid confrontation in the first place. So his hope was that he could bring this down a notch, enough so that they realized the hole they were digging for themselves.

"So how much you got?"

("Let's have it, *boi*.")

Despite himself, he was overcome with the urge to turn and demand Johnny think of a new epithet, that *boi* sounded stupid and did nothing but grate on his nerves.

Instead, he shrugged. "As much as you want." He locked eyes with Jimmy. "But my stuff's back at the van. Take me to it and I'll write you a check." Of course, there was no checkbook. He just needed Jimmy to respond. Any reply would do.

Johnny spoke first this time: "Oh you funny, *boi.*"

Devin cringed inwardly, strove to keep Johnny out of his head.

Jimmy said, "What kind o'—"

Devin exploded. Like a giant pair of blunt scissors, his right hand chopped the pulse of the knife-bearing wrist as his left hammered the back of the fist.

The wrist collapsed. The articular disc gave way. The ring finger metacarpal snapped. Even as the knife whirled through the night like an out-of-control helicopter, Devin shot an almost invisible right backfist to the bridge of Jimmy's nose. The bejeweled shades shattered.

At the same time, he grasped Jimmy's right with his left, thumb on the back of the hand, fingers on the pulse. He bent it toward Jimmy and torqued out, *hard.*

As the arm bent outward, he slammed his right forearm on the inside of Jimmy's elbow, looped it down then back up the front, the wrist now locked behind Devin's armpit, Jimmy's arm twisted around Devin's shoulder like a ruined Beetle Bailey paper clip.

In the next instant, he reached around Jimmy's head with his free hand and grasped a row of earrings. He torqued the kid's arm right, his head left—until he felt the cervical spine giving way.

Even as Devin pivoted, swinging the human shield into position, the pistol thundered.

Face grimaced in rage (was that what they called a "grill" across Johnny's teeth?), piece held sideways in classic gansta fashion, left hand grasping his crotch, Johnny punched the gun with every shot. A round slammed into the car. Another whined off the pavement. Then Jimmy shrieked (*uh-oh*) and spouts of gravel leapt from the side of the road. On and on, it seemed to last forever.

Click.

The reports called back from the hills. A flock of crows had taken wing over the cotton field, shadows scolding the blackened sky.

Dumbfounded, mouth agape, Johnny gawked at the pistol. The slide was stuck back. Smoke coiled from the muzzle. The poor dumb baby had probably never even fired the thing, much less given any forethought to what would happen if he did.

Jimmy wailed in pain. "My leg!" Devin felt him dancing on the pavement. "Mutha fucker shot me in my Goddamn *leg!*"

Johnny stared at his brother, at Devin—not at them but through them. His panting sounded like lumberjacks working at a crosscut saw on rain-soaked wood. He looked back at his hand, owl-eyed. He seemed mystified to discover a gun was in it.

He dropped the 9 as if it were scalding. Wiped his hand on his pants.

He turned on his heel, grasping a wad of crotch, and bumbled down the road in the headlight beams.

Devin released Jimmy. *"Damn* it!" The kid crumbled to the pavement with all the grace of an understuffed scarecrow.

And his pain finally kicked in. Cradling the mangled arm, curled in fetal position, Jimmy tilted his head back and screamed into the night.

Devin kicked the boy's back. "What the *hell,* Jimmy?" When the only reply was a yelp, he added, "What was that?" He kicked him again, harder. "*Huh?*" Before he kicked the boy a third time—then again and again until his leg gave out—he shook his head and turned away.

He paced the highway, fingers laced in his hair. Had he completely blown it here? How much trouble was this going to be? Sure as hell, blue lights would come flashing down the highway any minute.

Great. Perfect timing.

No doubt he'd end up cuffed and stuffed and bombarded with redundant questions, the cops deaf to his pleas.

Jimmy was keening like a sick kitten. Devin looked at him—then stopped looking at him. He gritted his teeth and kept pacing.

Of course, he'd acted only in self-defense. Fat chance Jimmy would back that. So what were his options here? Whatever he did, he needed to do it fast.

The punk sounded like a three-year-old who'd just been spanked, crying unabashedly now.

Devin remembered the scream during the fusillade. He sighed— "Let me see your leg." —and bent to the boy. "Move your hand."

Jimmy seemed not to hear him, kept rocking and keening.

"Move your fucking hand!"

The kid released his leg and clawed at the pavement instead.

Devin examined the wound. If the femoral artery was severed—even nicked—he'd need medical attention sooner than later. The neon light bleeding from beneath the car was dim at best. Still, he could see enough to determine the round had gone through and through, in and out the quadriceps. Apparently they'd loaded the gun with range rounds, for the exit wound showed no signs of bullet expansion. It was bleeding alright, but not pulsing.

Thank God.

He snared Jimmy's wrist and moved it back to his leg. "Press here." Then, "Jimmy, I need your car."

"Take it," the kid whined.

Devin stood.

Jimmy looked up at him, contorted face. "Don't kill me." He shook his head. "Please. Don't kill me man."

"Shut up!" Devin drew another yelp from the kid with a gut kick. "I'm not going to hurt you, dumbass. Not if you don't pull another *knife* on me." He punctuated *knife* with another kick.

Jimmy groaned and rolled into himself like a pill bug.

"Give me your phone."

Nothing.

"Phone Jimmy *phone!"* With some effort, he resisted dishing out another blow.

"Sun visor." Jimmy rolled his head, eyes squeezed shut. "Sun visor, man. Just take it."

"Okay listen up. When I roll out of here, I'm calling an ambulance for you. Cops always come with them, and I need you to tell them something. You listening?"

Jimmy nodded, eyes clenched shut.

"There were two murders." Grace's glassy eyes materialized before him. "At the Morrilton Piggly Wiggly." His voice broke.

He took a deep breath, blocking out the pain. "And a girl's been kidnapped, Jimmy. Tell them the reason I didn't wait around is because I'm going to try and catch up with them."

The kid seemed to be sleeping.

"You get all that?"

He just groaned.

"*I said you got that Jimmy?*"

"Yeah, yeah. I got it, man."

"And Jimmy." Devin's anger reignited. "Get your *life together!*" Another kick, this time right in the ass, hard enough to tweak Devin's ankle.

As he turned for the car, he gasped when he nearly bumped heads with a third punk.

Shit. Back seat.

The sucker punch shot out, but it wasn't even close.

Devin parried with his left and blasted a cross over the missed strike. The knuckles on meat sounded like a 2x4 whacking a fat steak.

The punk's head rocked back. He stumbled two steps, reflexively touched his mouth. Checked his fingers for blood. Scowled when he found it there. He lunged forward.

Devin had moved in as the punk teetered back. He kicked *down* into the baggie pants, shoved them to the ground.

Pants around his ankles, penis tip peeking through his boxers, the boy examined his predicament. He looked up just in time to see Devin complete a full 180 spin. The heel of the penny loafer slammed the left side of his head like a sledge hammer.

Devin surveyed the bone-heads, one out cold and the other writhing in pain. He took a step toward the car—then stopped.

How many shots had Johnny fired? A Glock 9 has a capacity of as many as sixteen rounds. Had he fired sixteen? Devin didn't think so, but it was hard to count bullets when they were flying at you.

He strode over to the pistol and scooped it up. The slide was back, but only partially. Not *locked* back. In the ejection port stood an empty shell casing. A stove-pipe, he thought he'd heard it called at the range.

Semi-automatic pistols require a trained hand with a firm grip in order to function properly. Johnny had likely never even fired the weapon, much less practiced with it. He'd had zero technique or control. This explained the stovepipe.

He relieved pressure from the slide, clearing the obstruction. Upon release, the slide completed its cycle, seating a bullet firmly in the chamber. He ejected the magazine, examining it as he turned for the car. Two more gleaming rounds.

He slammed the magazine back into the well and stuffed the gun in his waistband. A smile stole across his face: Armed and mobile, complete with a cell phone. Not bad.

"Tell them, Jimmy!" He ducked into the car and slammed the door.

━ ━

Jessi would always remember breaking her first board. It had looked so easy when she'd watch others do it; she'd wondered how anyone could *not* do it.

Until she stood staring at one.

Suddenly she was not so confident. She found herself doubting the technique, doubting her strength, even doubting Master Pastor's reassurances. She knew it was possible. Simple even. But theory and practice proved painfully different.

It occurred to her just how strong wood was. Tables were wooden, and some step ladders. Branches supported tree houses. Cars crashed into trees, leaving the hood mangled, the tree trunk no worse for the wear.

She shook out her hands—and realized the board holders' fingers seemed suddenly larger than the board itself. So easy to smash and bruise and break; she was certain she'd miss the board and plow instead into one of the straining digits, fingernails white with pressure.

Her eyes moved to their faces. One grimaced at the back of the board. The other looked directly at her. He nodded and tried to smile under his worry-line-wrinkled brow. Sweat poured down both faces.

She shook it off, chambered her elbow and shifted to a front stance.

Ready.

So, when to do it?

Now?

Or maybe *now?*

How about *now?*

Her arm dropped to her side. She shuddered and backed away.

That's how it was with the gun. The machine man was standing *right there in front of her!* He'd killed two people, one of them her mother. And now he threatened her. Bang the gavel, case closed, court adjourned.

So do it.

Now?

Or how about *now?*

Something slithered in her tummy. The gun shook in sympathy with her trembling hands. The stock felt slick; she was certain she'd drop it.

She tightened her grip, strengthening her resolve.

Her eyes floated up to his. Hazel with flecks of gray, they seemed kind. Peaceful.

Frightened.

He'd cleaned up his face and combed his hair. For her?

Stop it!

This creep cared about no one but himself. He'd probably washed his face so it would look better to him in the mirror.

So do it.

She had no more control of her trigger finger than she did of the stars in the sky.

Then Machine Man gave her a gift: He flinched. Perhaps the start of a lunge forward, perhaps just a nervous tick.

She squeezed the trigger like crushing a bug, tight and strong, sure and true, point blank, both barrels, squinting in anticipation of the thunder.

━ ━

Early this morning: Kutula "Tuli" Davis drove along sunny I-40 east, windows down, warm wind in her hair. Headed for Nashville. Back to school.

She glanced out over the cotton field bordering the highway. A flock of red wing black birds took to the sky, perhaps agitated by the dark clouds rolling in. She hoped she'd make it before the storm let loose.

Classes didn't start until Monday, but she just couldn't tolerate her family any longer. So she'd lied and claimed classes started tomorrow.

She had two choices: Sit behind the counter breathing redneck body stench, or smoke a little weed with her friends.

Hmmm. Tough choice.

She was already pie-eyed, big time. Not on weed. This was something else, something better. The high was a feeling of—what was it? Euphoria? Power? Who knew? Who cared? It was kicking her butt, and that's all that counted. From her left breast pocket, she extracted the source of the buzz. They seemed to transmit the feeling right through the shirt into her skin. She couldn't resist a giggle.

She hated to get rid of them; they were quite compact, yet the effect was so *potent!*

But her friends would disapprove. To say the least. Heck, they'd disown her if they found out she even knew where to get this junk.

Kutula was not her legal name. But her birth name was so disgusting, so embarrassingly stupid, she'd have wiped it from her memory if she could. Much less would she ever again *use* it.

Her legal name was *Dong,* the *g* more suggested than pronounced. At least that's what it sounded like when Paul Davis, her hillbilly father, said *Dawn.* And when *she* said the name—her *own name* (well, it used to be)—he accused her of pronouncing it *Don.* They'd argued last night at dinner (they called it supper) about the pronunciation, but the point was moot for two reasons: One, when someone who speaks actual English converses with someone who speaks redneck, the words *Dong, Don,* and *Dawn* are going to be unavoidably confused.

Two, her name was now Kutula.

Tuli, damn it! *Kutula* had meaning and a history, a name she could speak with pride.

It meant *peace* in the Fanagolo pidgin of South Africa. Fanagolo, she'd tried to explain to her ignorant family, was not a true language, but a pidgin, or a kind of trade dialect made up of more than one language. Of course, Paul couldn't resist joking about it, proclaiming "Don" had got her new name from a "pigeon."

Hopeless.

And that stupid store. What kind of name was *Toot-n-Moo,* for Christ's sake? What an embarrassment. She could just imagine the scene when they came up with it, all gathered around a card table one night, no doubt shit-faced, suggesting asinine southern expressions until someone shouted *"TOOT-N-MOO! YAAAAY!"*

She cringed at the thought of working the counter. All day and all night, farmers, rednecks, and just stupid ugly people dropped by for hunting and fishing supplies.

And to flirt with Ruth. Her mother.

She called her parents by their names. Ruth and Paul. She was, after all, twenty years old. An adult. In fact, a more conscientious adult than her parents, since she no longer indulged in the consumption of dead flesh. Naturally, Paul loved to trick her into eating bacon bits or something made with lard just to tease her.

Oh honey, don't pay him no mind. Ruth always tried to console her, to play it down. She never murdered or skinned or scaled the animals, but she did cook and serve them. That made her a willing accomplice.

Tuli grimaced. The men who strolled into the Toot-n-Moo expected her to flirt back like Ruth did. Were they kidding? *Flirt?* With those tobacco spitting, snaggletooth, gun toting imbeciles?

Oh but they tried: "How may I help you, Dong?" Then the dramatic pause. "HU HU HU! Why, I'z just reading your *name tag,* gorgeous!"

Ha ha.

And there was the old standby: "Honey, you got them pretty eyes like your mama's. Blue as Windex."

Windex. Nice.

But last night was where she drew the line. At the end of her shift, she'd knocked her water bottle to the floor. She'd snared a towel from beneath the counter . . .

This is why there was so much violence in the world. Every gun on earth should be melted down, encased in concrete and sunken to the bottom of the sea.

She recognized the shotgun. When Paul had gotten a new pump-action model for Christmas a few years back, he'd announced the retiring of this old relic. By *retire,* she hadn't realized he'd meant hacking it up and leaving it here—*here*—where she was forced to work—*like a slave*—within feet, sometimes inches of this instrument of *hate!* She'd thrown the towel back over it as if covering a snake, vowing to bend her parents' ears about it.

Then she thought of a better idea. She smirked as she carried out her plan.

As Paul had taken over, she'd skipped away humming.

"Finally takin' to workin' the counter, are ye?"

She just shot a wink over her shoulder and pushed through the door.

So now with a sigh, she tossed the two twelve-gauge shotgun shells out into the morning sun.

"Good riddance," she mumbled, and giggled again. They thought they were so tough. All Bonnie and

Clyde. But now the Toot-n-Moo back-counter was as safe as any preschool classroom.

In the aftermath of the events that would take place this very night, she'd finally nail down the feeling of the buzz.

She'd felt smug.

= =

Ka-Click.

Jessi's chin quivered. Her vision clouded and her breath hitched.

Machine Man smiled. "N' use common sense. It ain't got no *bullets* in it!" He snatched the gun away, then slammed it into her face.

She collapsed in a heap.

Chapter 4

Today I journey deeper in. I must distance myself from the abyss. I take nothing with me, for there are no possessions here. I don't know where I'll go—just far away from It.

The walls of darkness expand before me, allowing me to roam even as they envelop me. It dawns on me there is no time here. No morning, no light—only perpetual night.

How long have I traveled?

Minutes? Days?

Years?

They accompany me, the dead ones. They try, but they are no help. Nor are they even good company. I begin to suspect they are nothing but me, talking to myself.

I miss the voice. But she dwells only in the vicinity of the abyss.

Why is that?

Very suspicious.

Yet I trust her somehow.

Is she a protector? Can I survive without her? Should I consider turning back?

I panic at a realization. How can I retrace my steps—perhaps for miles—if I cannot see them? Perhaps I could feel my way.

I bend to test the ground and discover . . .

There is no ground.

Walls, ceiling, and floor of only darkness. What is this place?

Curiosity turns to panic as claustrophobia consumes me. What if It is not the only threat? What other impish creatures might lurk about? Small but savage, waiting crouched, beady-eyed or blind, designed for darkness, sharp teeth . . .

Hungry . . .

≃ ≃

Food. Good. Yes. Good food!

The beady-eyed Opossum stuffed its face with stale Chicken McNuggets, its head buried in the discarded bag. Enraptured by the cuisine, its eighteen inch bald rattail stood erect in the night air. He was all but oblivious of the neon blue ebb growing brighter by the second. He smacked and chewed, grunting and smacking.

The light grew brighter still.

Reluctantly, he stopped chomping. Listening.

Danger? Maybe . . . (Food. So good.) He sniffed the McNuggets and opened his mouth to dig in again.

No wait. Strange light.

Groaning resentfully, he extracted his crummy face from the treasure chest. He sniffed and searched—up on his haunches now—sniffed and studied, unable to completely free his mind from the midnight snack.

Bright lights approached. Coming in fast. *(Food. Mmmmm.)* A mechanical scream filled the night. It rose in pitch, then plummeted as it shrieked by with a burst of air that parted his tummy fur.

Hmph. Maybe I should move? Uh . . . should have *moved? (Food.) Play dead? Nah. Too late.*

Had he been able to read, he'd have enjoyed the airbrushed message on the passenger side of the vehicle: *2 Hot 2 Handle.* He did note that the scream-thing was the color of fire.

Fire. Dangerous.
(Food.)
Fire hot.
(FOOD.)
Danger?
FOOOOOD!

━ ━

Inside the low-rider, tearing down the Old Conway Highway, Devin tossed a smoldering roach out the cracked window. A 7-11 bag billowed lazily over the passenger's seat, whispering plastic secrets.

He spied a small open cooler on the back seat. Ice water barely covered a Coors. He imagined the crushed empties dotted the highway like breadcrumbs leading back to the source of the beer.

He snared the bag mid-flight, then carefully moved the cooler to the front, being sure to stay between the lines whizzing by outside.

Straining the cubes with his fingers, he fashioned an ice pack. What he needed was ibuprofen. Not to mention rest. What he *really* needed was an x-ray.

What he had was half-melted ice in a leaky 7-11 bag. So he twisted the top, then pressed the dripping wad to his ribs.

He flipped down the sun visor and the promised cell phone fell into his lap.

He picked it up. Bounced it in his hand.

What, exactly, was he supposed to say to the cops?

Hello, this is Devin James and I . . . Excuse me? Jimmie Whitlock? Oh. I'm calling from his phone. In fact, I'm driving his car, too. Where is he? Oh, he's lying on the Old Conway highway. Bleeding from a bullet wound. No no, I didn't shoot him. I was busy ripping him in half while his brother shot him. Then I took his car and phone. With permission, of course. And oh yeah—I fled the scene of a kidnapping in Morrilton. You'll find two bodies back there and . . . What's that? Oh no, I didn't shoot them, either. And no, I don't have the girl. A machine-man dressed like a junior-high metal-head took her.

Anywhooo, you'll find me flying down the Old Conway Highway at about 110 miles per hour, just past the . . . Hmmm?

No, he'd have to think this out.

Although he was the pastor, it was always Vivian who guided him back to God. When things got messy, he found men tended to try and hash through it on their own. But women never seemed to mind consulting the directions.

Vivian spoke softly to him now, and so he shook his head and prayed.

He was supposed to open with thanks. Anyone knew that. But what did he have to be thankful for? His ribs all but hobbled him. Jessi was stuffed in a trunk headed God-knows-where. And two of his friends lay stiffening back at the Piggly Wiggly.

When he thought about it, he supposed he could be lying dead back there himself had it not been for the bible. But was that God or just dumb luck? Probably dumb luck.

And if God was pulling the strings up there, why had He stuck him with this ridiculous ride? Begrudgingly, he admitted that, while 2-Cold-2-Hold-2-Hot-2-Handle would not have been his first choice for transportation, it was certainly a *fast* car, and definitely beat the heck out of running after the killer.

He sighed, then relinquished his gratitude for his meager blessings. To his own ear, he sounded like a ten-year-old coerced into apologizing to his younger sister: *Sooor-ryyyy*. He didn't even bother asking forgiveness for his shortcomings. God knew what they were; hell, He'd been the one who baked them into him. Besides, where would he even start?

He asked for guidance concerning the conversation he needed to have with the police—and flipped open the phone.

PLEASE ENTER ACCESS CODE: _ _ _ _

"You have *got* to be kidding me." He punched 9-1-1. Surely the phone would process an emergency call, even when locked. He pressed ENTER. He was re-warded with only an admonishing

BEEP!

and the reasserted message

PLEASE ENTER ACCESS CODE: _ _ _ _

He sat staring at the screen, flummoxed.

Wasn't there a law or something that required emergency calls be available, even from a locked phone? Of course, even if that were the case, Jimmy would probably have figured a way around it, lest he inadvertently butt-dial the police in the middle of ne-gotiating a deal on a bag of weed.

His upper lip twitched and his jaws clenched. He took a shot at guessing the code. WWJD came to mind. In this case, that stood for, *What Would Jim-mie Dial?* Instead, he entered

6 6 6 6

BEEP!

PLEASE ENTER ACCESS CODE: _ _ _ _

Okay, no worries. Just try another one.

Sweat beaded on his brow.

In counseling teens, he'd run across the number 420, which was supposedly the police code for a mari-juana violation—or maybe April 20th was pot day somewhere. Something like that. Whatever the case, he knew it was 420.

0 4 2 0

BEEP!

PLEASE ENTER ACCESS CODE: _ _ _ _

4 2 0 0

BEEP!

PLEASE ENTER ACCESS CODE: _ _ _ _

Alright, maybe the idiot hadn't even programmed a number.

0 0 0 0

BEEP!

PLEASE ENTER ACCESS CODE: _ _ _ _

"Come. *On!*" Okay, what other numbers might interest a little punk gansta-wannabe-be? How about *2112,* the title of a Rush album? Okay, from like a hundred years ago, but still.

2 1 1 2

BEEP!

PLEASE ENTER ACCESS CODE: _ _ _ _

Drive back and beat the code out of Jimmy?
No. He was already on borrowed time.
He could always start at 0001 and work his way up
to 9999.

"Shit shit *shit!*" He hammered the phone against
the wheel. *"Jimmy you pathetic little—"*
The road fired white-dash tracer rounds under the
hood. His stomach lurched. He cut right. The wheel
proved sensitive to even a feather touch; the dashes
moved left, then *too* far left, firing white slashes seemingly into another galaxy. His skin flashed icy hot
when gravel sprayed the undercarriage.
Tires screeching, ice-water in his veins, he finally
got it back on the road.
After an eternity, he registered the screaming engine. He realized he was panting. The spectral beams
out front seemed to illuminate an alternate version of
the recent past: a twirling world of crushed cotton
plants, exploding glass, black sky, blood.
He did not pray. His mind went blank. He just
breathed through his nose, teeth clenched, and
pounded the little racecar for all it was worth, engine
revving like a UFO out of hell.

— —

The retching rip of packing tape still rang in his ears. The clear strips disfigured her lips and twisted her skin, an ugliness he found somehow . . . pretty.

Loveless stood transfixed, one hand propped on the trunk lid. Bunny's nose. Chipped sparkle polish on bitten nails. Delicate ear like a pink rose bud tinseled in blond . . .

And that *ponytail!*

That was it, that was the sign. She was The One. Even when the shotgun was on him back there, he'd had no fear. What better way to go than lost in her eyes?

As he folded in behind the wheel, he wondered if maybe he'd bound her too tight. He only meant to teach her a lesson. Like she was grounded. He didn't want to hurt her none. Maybe he'd check on her in a little while.

He started the car and pulled out onto the highway.

It was a ways yet to Butcher's Gap, the best deer hunting land in Arkansas, maybe the entire south. A nice peaceful place to have their talk. Then maybe, just maybe—begin their life together.

They'd roll in about sunup.

He had a good scheme going and was right proud of it. He never hunted in his own backyard of Jameson, not ten miles east of Butcher's Gap. No, what he did was hunt circles around Conway, clear across the state from home. He'd select towns outside Conway, but never Conway itself. So if the cops ever picked up on a Missing Little Mary pattern—which the bumbling Barney Fife fucks wouldn't, but if they did—the center of the kidnappings, and thus the focus of their search, would be Conway, not Jameson.

Like ole Coach Tanner used to say: *Always be thinkin'*.

He chuckled.

He never used his own ride. How stupid would that be? Why no, he just lifted one, then returned it before the owner even knowed it was gone. That way he avoided a pattern developing. Like tire tracks and shit. He did his homework, oh yes he did. Watched every episode of C.S.I.

And if he had to make a run for it, why flash his tags out there like a whitetail deer? If he got away in a stolen car, they might trace it back to Jameson, but that's as close as they'd ever get.

And if he couldn't shake them? Well, he'd give 'em the best Bonnie-n-Clyde show they ever seen. Wouldn't nobody ever take him alive.

With three stiffs in his wake, they was liable to finally get off their asses and let the dogs out. Might start catching on to his scheme. That sucked. He'd have to ditch Conway as his pivot point—maybe even try a town in Tennessee. Shit, probably best to lay off altogether for a while.

And maybe he could. Maybe he could lay off forever because . . .

Maybe this was The One.

Senior Year: The disappearance of Mary Maples rocked the foundation on which Tim's life was built. His rage at the world was a pressure cooker, the relief valve high school football. Out on the field, he could hit something, hit some*one—hurt* someone—and nobody would say a thing about it. In fact, his aggression earned him praise. Even when he overdid it.

He remembered ole Coach Tanner's wisdom on the subject of cheating: *Just brang 'em the pork, boys. Once they eatin' bacon, don't nobody never worry how the hog got slaughtered.*

Through his senior year, Tim lived alone. No one even noticed. He remembered ole Gus's parting words as they stood over Mama's casket:

"You best forget her."

Tim looked over at him, perplexed.

Daddy answered his unasked question. "That Mary." His eyes never left the casket. "She a black widow spider, boy."

Tim glared at him, his grief now tainted with his anger, both overshadowed by his fear.

The old man just stared down at the corpse. He was an ape in a suit—face of cracked leather, dirty gray ponytail shedding dandruff on the black blazer. Tim thought maybe he'd checked out.

His eyes fell back to his mom.

"They all bitches."

Tim looked at him again.

"Ever' one." The old man's voice broke when he added, "Even your mama." He wiped his eyes roughly with his sleeve and sniffed, instantly composed himself. "Hell, 'specially your mama."

Junior Year: Tim loathed Fridays, which stood in the shadow of the looming weekend. All day Saturdays, his chest felt cinched, like he couldn't seem to get enough *air*. Sundays he spent blue-faced, desperate for breath—all clocks and springs, tripwires and triggers, like Monday might never come.

Mondays brought peace. Clarity. Mondays brought life at last.

Because Mondays meant Mary. The moment he laid eyes on her, even from across campus, his breaths came in mighty rejuvenating waves, filling him, calming him.

But Mondays were a blur. And Tuesdays and Wednesdays. On Thursdays, he constantly had to remind himself the week wasn't over yet; he had two more days of easy breathing.

This Shadow Friday was especially dark, the last game-day of the year. Basketball season would follow, then track, during both of which Tim would fade to anonymity, just another damn country boy wandering the halls.

Lunchtime was drawing to a close. He stood watching her from across the smoking lot, as he had been for the better part of the hour. Mary sat under a tree reading, the fall breeze teasing at her hair. Every flipping of a page seemed to cast into history yet another hour since they'd spoken, the tight stack of pages a closed book of days—of weeks and months and years—all sealed in the papery past.

Sadness overcame him. Smothered him. Scared him. He didn't know what to do with that.

He gritted his teeth. Sucked three big breaths, blew them out through his nose like a racehorse.

He was no sissy; he wasn't sad. Just frustrated. He clenched his fists, pounding his frustration into anger.

Now anger was something he could work with.

He shoved off the wall and strode toward the tree. He didn't know what he planned to say, but by God he'd say *something*. He'd spent his last airless weekend. Summer would be here before you knew it, and he refused to spend it pining away like some sick damn puppy.

As he neared, his anger dissipated, and his resolve. He could no more retrieve it than he could grasp a wisp of smoke.

He found himself at the tree, blocking out Mary's sunlight. He couldn't seem to swallow.

She'd grown. How had he missed that? The freckles were still there, evident even in his shadow, but her cherub face was chiseled now, like a face you'd see in a Calgon commercial.

With some effort, he drew a breath.

She peered up at him. "Why they . . . Tim Loveless." She set down her book and stood. Her smile was warmer than the sunlight. "Let me take a look at you now." She stepped back, shading her eyes, looking him over. "Football star, great big ole four-wheel-drive truck, all grown up . . . "

More than her words, it was the *way* she talked. By God, that's what he loved about Mary. She knew how to calm him, yet make him feel strong. Like he *was* somebody. "As a matter of fact, I'z wondering if maybe you wanted to take a ride in that four-wheel-drive. Maybe tonight after the game."

She squinted, just ever so slightly. And did her shoulders fall? Like she was disappointed or something?

Tim looked at his feet and shoved his hands in his pockets. He found a stone on the ground, kicked it.

"Alright, Tim."

He looked up, astonished.

"Tonight after the game. I'll meet you by your truck."

He slowly nodded, resisted doing a somersault right there in the grass. "Well alright then."

She nodded back— "It's a date." —gathered her things, and headed off to class.

He stood watching her go. After all these years, a date. A *date* with Mary Maples! And all he had to do was just walk up and ask. Why hadn't he done it years ago?

The game was a blur. Time stood still yet leaked as if from a sieve. All he could think about was freckles and frolicking with Mary, of books of better days packed with pages of the future.

Finally somehow, they were alone in the truck.

She did all the talking. He was fine with that; he didn't have much to tell, anyway. He thought, *I could live like this.*

She went on about classes and college plans. Shared some family stories. She even got around to

Kitty Hackett, who'd died of cancer just last year. Nobody missed her.

"Old Battle Ax," Tim finally contributed.

Mary laughed and went on jabbering.

As they neared the old dirt road—more of a mud rut passable only in a four-wheel-drive—a mischievous grin stole across his face. The entrance was all but hidden if you didn't know what you was looking for. Mary was sure to be surprised.

"Hold on!" He swung the wheel hard right.

It looked like ole Mary's heart caught in her throat. Tim chuckled as they bounced through the ditch. Mary pinned her hands to the ceiling and braced her feet on the dash.

The road was constantly changing due to neglect, weather, and undergrowth. Even with off-road vehicles, more than a few got theirself stuck. If that happened, the only way to get *un*stuck was a bumper-mounted winch. If you had one.

Tim did.

Her squeals of delight warmed his heart. He'd been dreaming of this his whole life.

Into creeks, around boulders, over underbrush and through puddles like ponds they bounded, gyrating like a circus ride. The engine was a tub-voiced giant grumbling in protest. Saplings scraped the undercarriage. Metallic banging from the bed-mounted toolbox. The headlight beams were twin ghosts cleaving the darkness, seemingly clearing the way.

After fifteen minutes or so, he found an open place in the trail.

He skidded to a stop. The truck sat idling, still swaying in memory of the ride, seemingly prancing and pawing like a crazed bronco working off its panic.

"Ooooee!" Mary exclaimed.

Tim killed the engine.

"That is without a doubt the most fun I've had since grade school!" Her chest heaved. She looked over at him. "Maybe *ever!*"

"I'm real proud you enjoyed it."

As she caught her breath, a comfortable silence fell between them. The only sounds were the pinging of the engine and the echo of whippoorwills in the distance. The cab was dark, illuminated only by canopy-filtered moonlight.

Minutes passed.

Tim began to wonder what to do. He looked over at her lap, at her hands folded there. He imagined holding one, just like old times. All he had to do was reach over and take it.

He didn't do it. Couldn't. He sent the signal to his arm, but it refused to budge. What was he so scared of? Why did she seem so out of reach? It was like there'z a big ole damn brick wall between them. Invisible, but solid as the walls of a prison cell.

Was it her? Was it him? Had he done something wrong? Said something stupid? Maybe he shoulda got her flowers or something.

He heard himself say, "Mary, I—"

"Shhhh . . . Listen." A whisper. "Isn't that the most beautiful sound you've ever heard?"

He creased his brow. *What is she talking about?*

"Let's just sit here. Let's just *be* for a minute."

He didn't understand. What did she mean, *be?* What beautiful sound? Wasn't nothing out there but critters. No music, nothing like that. Maybe she was hearing things.

Or delaying. Maybe Mary was scared of that big ole wall much as he was.

By God, he'd break it down for both of them.

He leaned to kiss her. After all these years, their first kiss.

She pursed her lips and stiffened. Pushed him away. "Now hold your horses a minute, Tim."

She all the sudden seemed to forget the airs she'd put on over the years. He discovered he liked that. He didn't mind her fancy talk—but this was much better, her talking natural like everybody else.

"This is been coming for some time now, I guess. And maybe I should have said something before but—" She sighed and shook her head. "You and me? We been knowin' each other since grade school. I can't say I ain't noticed you taking a interest in me during all them years but . . . well, it ain't you, see. Just, I don't want to be interested in nobody." She shook her head and scoffed. "I mean, anybody."

She didn't seem to know what to do with her hands. What was she so scared of?

"Besides, all this time we known each other? Heck, we're more like kin than anything else, don't you think?"

The ground seemed to drop from beneath him. Like they was ridin' his ole four-wheel-drive right down out the sky.

"Right?" After a beat, she repeated, "Right, Tim?"

His vision blurred and his chin quivered. He turned to the windshield, stared out at the wooded world beyond. Violence waited around every tree and rock out there, ever patient, poised to pounce at your slightest slip. Wasn't nothing different about this world.

"Look at me, Tim."

He turned to her. His heart sank. She was so beautiful; she was . . . *perfect*. And she was *right there!* His for the taking.

But yet . . . she was as far away as any constellation in the night sky.

"You're my special friend," she pleaded. She shook her head. Smiling. Like she was offering some kind o' damn consolation prize.

She just didn't see it, that's all. He'd show her. Help her understand. She was his *Mary*.

His Mary.

He bent to kiss her again.

She struck at his granite shoulders, kicking and squirming, squeals muted between their lips.

He scooted forward, bore his weight down on her. He would *make* her understand. She was his and he was hers, each the other's only escape from this hellhole town, this miserable life.

She kept flailing, struggled harder still.

This disappointed him—but also excited him somehow. He'd demonstrate his strength to her. In fact, maybe that's what she was asking for, what she needed to see.

He'd show her he could protect her. He'd do *anything* for her—lie, cheat, steal, or kill for her. Whatever it took. If only he could make her *see*.

She bit his lip.

He pulled away and bolted upright. Wiped at the dribble on his chin. Examined his fingers. The smears looked like dirty motor oil in the darkness.

He looked back at her, stunned.

She slapped him.

"What the *hell*, Tim! Here I am trying to talk to you like a human being, trying to share my feelings with you and—"

He kissed her again.

She kicked and squirmed, this time outright screaming in his mouth, fists and knees useless under his bulk.

And she bit him again.

This time, he bit her back.

When her struggles only escalated, his frustration turned to anger, his anger to rage. He bellowed through clenched teeth, her lower lip between them, and shook his head like a pit bull, biting harder still.

With a rip like tearing the hide from a squirrel, they parted.

He sat up.

Something cloyed in his mouth.

He spit reflexively; it splatted on the dashboard.

Indeed blood, but something else, too.

Something . . . thicker.

When he looked back at Mary, she was fingering her mouth. *Tearing* at it. Rocking in pain.

Her hands eased away as if of their own accord. Trembling. Smeared with dirty oil.

Tim's breath caught in his throat. His blood pooled in his feet.

She shrieked. Flailed her hands hysterically.

He turned his gaze to the windshield. "Love me." His chin quivered.

She only screamed, squirming in place like a worm on a hook.

"Love me!"

But she wasn't Mary anymore. Writhing beside him now was an injured animal, a gut-shot deer, bellowing babble, making no kind of sense at all.

He turned back to her— *"Love me!"* —and slapped her face.

She didn't seem to feel it, or even to hear him.

"LOVE ME!" He throttled her neck. He had to snap her out of this, wake her up, make her *see.*

"LOVE ME!"

He bashed her head against the window ledge.

"LOVE ME!"

Again and again, each slam sounded like a brick smashing a windshield.

"LOVE ME!"

Mist of blood—

"LOVE ME!"

Struggles fading—

"LOVE ME!"

And her screams . . .

The forest was a stage upon which unseen creatures enacted a play. Glee and terror, order and chaos, life and death. Both peaceful and infuriating—but inexorable, never-ending.

By day, capricious wrens and sparrows chirruped and cheeped, twittering in the branches. Fattening up for winter migration.

Sometimes by day, but mostly at night, desperate cries of a mother jay pierce the peace as she witnesses the consumption of her children. Stealthy, sleek, and iron strong, the black racer's eyes are lidless. Expressionless, it only stares as the warm pink morsels slide down its throat. It all but ignores the laments of the mother. But if she ventures too close, well, the snake is happy to put an end to her suffering.

Listening, Loveless is kneeling, oblivious of the mud soaking through his jeans.

Rocking. Mindless.

Mary lies before him, bloody bib, glassy stare, heinous grin.

He closes his eyes and travels back to fourth grade, where Little Mary, holding *his* hand, sought *his* shelter, *his* peace. Freckled nose . . . knobby knees . . . silken ponytail.

He opens his eyes and there is the other Mary. Staring into the ether. Lower teeth exposed like a skull.

"You ain't her." His voice breaks.

(*They's* lots *of Marys, Timmy.*)

"Not. My. *Mary.*" Gritted teeth. Snarl slick with tears.

(*There she'll be, in all her glory,* your *Mary . . .*)

"You ain't her."

He stands. After a moment, he nudges the carcass over with his boot.

Much better.

He picks up the shovel . . . and pauses.

No choice but to let her go now. Except . . .

The silky blond ponytail shimmers like a talisman, the very source of the light of the moon.

He stands transfixed. After an eternity, he blindly slips the hunting knife from his boot.

Yes, this will be nice. He won't have to let her go after all.

Not all of her.

Tim Loveless stared out the windshield.

Mama stared back. (*They's* lots *of Marys, Timmy.*)

"Did I finally find her?" His voice shook. "I been lookin' real hard." His breath hitched. "Is it her?" He strained his ear for an answer—for a whisper, a breath, anything. "Can you tell me?" When his voice cracked, he took a calming breath and bit back a sob.

His vision clouded. "I'm tired, Mama. Real tired." He swiped his eyes with a sleeve.

He admitted to himself a terrible truth. Her face had been fading. Even old class pictures seemed to change somehow; only paper people stared back at him, strangers he'd never known.

Even Mary.

How could he search if he no longer knew what he was looking for?

How could he go on?

The clock was out, the game was done, the ball was in the air. This was it, his Hail-Mary pass, his last and only hope. All he had—what he absolutely depended on—was that the perky Little Mary in the trunk was different from the others.

She was tough. That was a good sign. Sweet, too— and looked like his Mary. From what he could remember.

She made him feel . . . something.

She made him *feel.*

━━ ━━

"Stop it!"

Mike and Mark Owen stood staring back at Grace, looking like two cats caught killing the canary. It wasn't far from the truth. A wren had fluttered into the house. The men had been trying unsuccessfully to capture it. Despite Jessi's protestations, they'd resorted to "gently" pinning it down with brooms. Except the brooms were beginning to look like giant hammers, the bird a feathered nail.

"Sit!" Grace jabbed her finger at the couch.

They plopped down, one on either side of Jessi.

The bird perched in a corner, panting with fatigue. Its tiny feet clung to the vertical trim running up the wood-paneled wall.

Grace turned to it. "Hey there." She all but sang the words, a lullaby.

The bird looked at her, beak open, seemingly prepping for launch.

"It's ok, baby. You just rest."

Trembling, it scanned the room with tiny jerks of its head, one eye always on the woman.

"No one's going to hurt you now."

It fixed again on Grace as she eased cautiously forward. Jessi watched in awe.

After a time (and how did she decide when it was time?), Grace slowly extended her arm, one finger held sideways—and inched closer still.

Jessi's dad shook his head and glanced over at Uncle Mark.

She didn't know how long it had been, but somehow her mother had closed the distance. Her finger hovered right at the feathered breast. Jessi gasped when the wren hopped onto it, then stretched its wings.

Grace stood with it, cooing and air-kissing as if she had all day. Still consoling, she turned slowly for the sliding glass door. Jessi scampered over and slid it open. She looked back at the men. They sat stunned, both jaws sagging like a couple of comic country gargoyles. Jessi smiled.

Out in the yard, her mother spoke matter-of-factly to the wren, as if this were an everyday thing, as if any bird would just fly up and sit on anyone's finger.

When it was ready, the bird crouched like a bunched spring, ready for take-off. After one final glance at its new friend, it leapt away and flitted off into the woods.

Jessi smiled up at her mother.

Mom looked down at her, blood-caked teeth behind lips of alabaster. "It's okay, baby." Her cataracted eyes rolled in her skull. "No one's going to hurt you now."

Screaming. Muted somehow, perhaps drowning chain-wrapped at the bottom of a lake. Her heart raced; her eyes snapped wide open.

No, not under water. Her mouth was sealed shut. She gasped desperately for breath through her nose.

Jessi realized where she was. The cramped space, the blood-red glow.

Lying on her side, she tried to move, but her arms and legs wouldn't seem to work. She rolled onto her back. Examined her arms. Her eyes widened.

Her forearms were bound in clear packing tape tinted red in the taillights' glow. The binding ran from her wrists down to almost her elbows. Veins bulged on her hands; her fingers were hooked. A glance down at her legs proved they'd suffered the same fate.

Just to be sure, she touched her lips.

Packing tape.

She closed her eyes, sighed through her nose and let her head fall back.

The dream had been not only a dream, but a memory. A real event, every detail. Except for its rude awakening.

To Jessi, Mom was just Mom. But she'd been more than that, hadn't she? People admired Grace Owen. With a few, it seemed their admiration was tinged with the slightest hint of . . . was it fear? Not often, but sometimes, people talked. Spoke in hushed tones. *(A touch of the seer in her.)* Jessi had never paid them much mind. But now a terrible truth punched her in the gut, stole her breath away. She'd never appreciated who her mother was, had she? Not really. She'd never asked about how she did the curious things she sometimes did. What she wouldn't give for just five more minutes with her. *Just five minutes!* Her chin trembled and her eyes clouded.

Stop it!

Whatever Mom was, she had zero patience for whining. Maybe that's why she and Dad had gotten on so well with Master Pastor. He had no time for the baby stuff, either.

She gritted her teeth and drew a deep breath.

Sensei had a whole library of stories about how to deal with all kinds of stuff. Multiple attackers, larger opponents, compensating for injuries . . . heck, he'd once done half a class on how to fight a *dog!*

But he'd never mentioned packing tape. A chuckle escaped her, imagining him wrapping some poor kid up like a mummy for a black belt test.

What Master Pastor did mention—in fact lectured on it all the time—was using your noodle. *Learning to fight is great, but it's the fighting spirit that counts. A survival scenario may not even involve kicking and punching. But you can always use the ability to stay calm in a pinch, just like when you're sparring. The most important thing you can do is to* think. *What if you're in a car accident? Or lost? Or find yourself flailing in a river?*

Or wrapped in packing tape.

She shook her head, staring at the trunk lid. Okay, so what did she know about packing tape?

She and her mother often volunteered at the church. One day, their work had included unpacking UPS boxes. Her mother had deftly opened them using only a ball point pen. She'd put a little pressure on the lid, as if trying to force it open, then perforate the tape along the seal until *pop!* the whole thing just snapped free.

So. Ball point pen? Fat chance of finding one in here. Much less a box cutter. Well, what else might work? Surely in the trunk of a car she could find something pointy enough to perforate packing tape. She hoped so, because her hands were beginning to feel like they were hosting ant races. The good news was, Machine Man had bound them in front. But the bad news was that they were numb—and growing more so by the minute.

She rolled to her elbows and knees. She felt like a Muslim bowing to Mecca. She hopped and scooted, squinting and feeling.

No good. In the dim light, she quickly lost track of where she'd been already.

She bumbled to the left front corner, right behind the seat back, then ran her hands along the felt, all the way to the taillight.

Her eyes were watering. Something tickled her sinuses. A breath drew of its own accord followed instantly by a sneeze. With her mouth sealed off, she was glad she hadn't blown her brains out her ears. Who knows what kind of dust she was stirring up? Pollen, cat hair, felt particles, beech sand. She thought about all the things Machine Man might have thrown back here over the years. Then she stopped thinking about it.

She backed up a scoonch and started the other direction. Back and forth she searched, patiently, like mowing grass or watering a garden.

Midway through the trunk, she struggled around to face the opposite direction and continued scanning.

About halfway across, she stopped. Something jutted from under the felt. This had to be what had been poking her earlier.

With a little more scanning, she located a seam: the spare tire cover. She lifted it and tossed it open.

Glowing red in the taillights, crammed down into the wheel disc of a filthy spare tire, an L-shaped tire tool. She grasped it, wrestled it free. She replaced the cover and rolled onto her back, then examined the tool.

On one end, the lug wrench. The other was flattened, probably for prying loose hubcaps. Blunt, not nearly as sharp as a pen—but maybe it would work.

She discovered she could sit upright if she ducked her head. She jammed the lug-wrench end between her thighs and braced it on the floor, the hubcap pry jutting up at her.

She sawed the tape across the blunt point.

No good.

She tried hammering her arms into it.

The hubcap pry was simply not sharp enough.

She yanked the tire tool free and tossed it into a corner. A scan of the rest of the compartment revealed butkus.

She rolled once more to her back, her head butted against the rear seat. Her knees ached. Her hands were throbbing. The tape encircling her head pulled painfully at her hair.

Master Pastor had this thing about what he called "pain noises." According to him, complaining just made things worse, focused your thoughts on the pain. But the trick wasn't to try and not think of it. When you tried to *not* think of something, you first had to think of what you were trying not to think of. The secret, he said, was to simply focus on something else.

She closed her eyes, took a calming breath—and let her mind wander.

The Drawing Wall.

Taekwondo class.

The tire swing Dad had hung from an ancient oak out back. She'd spent practically her whole life in that tree—climbing, exploring, swinging . . . sometimes she spun in circles on the swing, gazing upward, watching the canopy twirl against the endless sky.

Sometimes on cool nights of fall and spring, she'd camped under the tree with her mother. "Just us girls," Mom always said. They laid awake until they couldn't hold their eyes open, talking girl talk, talking about anything they pleased.

Just us girls.

Sometimes they counted shooting stars. One night Mom introduced her to the constellations. There of course the Big Dipper, which made up the body and tail of Ursa Major, the Big Bear. Always by her side was Little Bear, Ursa Minor, the body and tail of which formed the Little Dipper. Visible only in the spring were Cancer, Hydra and Virgo. In fall there was Andromeda and Pegasus. She always had trouble finding Pegasus; Mom would lie head to head with her, holding her hand, tracing the horse with their fingers.

She reached up and traced it now, in the night sky of her imagination. First the tail . . . no wait, you have to imagine the tail.

Her finger slid along the pressboard above her.

Front legs. Yes, the stars make up the front legs and . . .

Something blocked her finger. She examined it blindly with her hands.

A strip of trim.

She beetled her brow. A strip of trim would most likely be secured with . . .

She ran her hand along the wood, lightly lest she come across a splinter—not that a splinter was anything to worry about at the moment.

A screw head. Counter-sunk into the wood.

She scooted over a space, running her hands along the board until—another screw head. She scooted yet again, feeling, praying . . .

She released a pent-up breath.

One of the screws had either run into something metal, or maybe the jostling of the car had worked it loose over the years. Whatever the case, she had about a quarter inch to work with. Though it took some doing, she managed to work it maybe a half turn. But a half-turn tighter or a half-turn looser?

Into her mind flashed a time she'd helped Dad fix his truck. Well, she hadn't really helped. She knew that now. But he was nice about it, allowed her to hand him tools. She remembered a snippet of conversation:

How do you know which way to turn the bolts, Daddy?

Righty-tighty, lefty-loosey.

She turned the screw left. After only a little ways, it stuck. She invested a round to the right, then back to the left—wiggled it, shook it, calmly at first, then faster and harder as the minutes ticked by. She could have used her jacket to pad her fingers, only it was lying back at the Toot-n-Moo, soaked in the nice lady's blood.

She realized she was keening. Whimpering. Had the Machine Man heard?

Either he heard or he didn't. Just keep working.

The screw retreated another quarter inch. She pinched even harder, shaking and twisting. It seemed to be working, but she couldn't be sure.

Her fingertips were bruised. When a slickness formed on the metal, she told herself it was sweat, but she knew better.

Another quarter inch—she could move it side-to-side now.

Come on, come on . . .

The screw bounced from her taped lips into her hair. She grasped it in fingers that felt like cold sausages and began perforating along her lip line.

P-HHHHHH! She inhaled the stink of the trunk as if it were a fresh spring breeze.

Now her hands, thank the Lord.

She stuffed the head of the screw into her mouth.

She might as well have been wearing boxing gloves; the screw fell through her teeth and lodged in her throat. She gagged, hacked, reached carefully into her mouth and teased it out.

She imagined the morning headlines: *Girl chokes to death on screw, robbing kidnapper of pleasure of mutilating her.*

She bowed to Mecca once more, gravity now on her side, and grasped the screw in her teeth. Guiding the threaded shaft with her lips, she pushed it into the tape, right between her wrists.

The needle-sharp point broke through— "Ow!" — and jabbed the inside of her arm. A warm trickle worked its way between her wrists.

This wasn't going to be pretty. By the time she freed herself, her arms would look like a couple of tomatoes someone had used as pin cushions.

She kept working.

= =

The house was dark and silent. The refrigerator compressor kicked on, deafening in the stillness.

Forty-nine-year-old David Hayes loved the serene predawn morning. This time of day was made for him. Nice and quiet. Peaceful. Yet deceptively powerful. Morning was his opportunity to pray and meditate, a chance to reconnect with himself, to charge his spiritual batteries for the coming day.

Admiring his well-maintained back yard from the kitchen window, he sipped black coffee, careful to avoid his thick trim mustache. The calloused fingers gripping the cup handle barely fit.

Times were tough for an independent plumber in Jameson, but he'd make it. He'd do whatever he had to do for Daniel. The boy stirred even now, a few minutes before his alarm was to sound. David beamed with pride just listening to him wake up.

With their height and sinewy build, the Hayes could have been direct descendants of President Abraham Lincoln. More compelling evidence of such a pedigree were their quiet dispositions, soulful eyes and unusually large ears. There was no hiding the fact these were good hardworking country boys.

Before Daniel, David had never given death much thought. It was just something that came with the package. But with the birth of the boy fourteen years ago, his life took on a whole new meaning. Served a higher purpose. He'd quit dipping Copenhagen and sworn off the suds. He visited the doctor regularly, something he dreaded but did religiously nonetheless.

Because no one on this earth would ever understand Daniel like David did. A surrogate father may support him, even grow to love him—but no other man could *be* him. They were flesh and blood, the same soul in two bodies.

They never said, *I love you*. Those type feelings were better demonstrated than voiced. Even the thought of such talk directed his mind to other, more practical matters.

Like deer hunting.

The conversation more continued than started, the first words Daniel's as he shuffled into the kitchen in sock feet and orange camo pants. "Did I mention Sergeant Collins let me help teach the other boys to neutralize a firearm?" He opened the refrigerator and reached for the milk.

"Oh yeah? How'd that go?"

David had entered his son in the Junior Rangers program, which introduced young men to the world of law enforcement. They even went on Drive-Arounds with on-duty deputies. Parents had no concern with this, since the crime rate in Jameson had hovered at precisely zero since anyone could remember.

"Very well, actually."

David resisted a smile when Daniel's voice cracked, the boy's Adam's apple like a peach-fuzz fishing bobber.

"The other boys were impressed I already knew how to do it." Daniel poured a glass of milk. "One mistake they kept making was forgetting to check the breech. They remembered to eject the magazine, but nobody checked the breech."

David had taught the boy gun safety since Daniel was big enough to hold one up. Hunting was a way of life for them, as it had been for generations. They kept loaded firearms around their home without concern. First, Daniel could handle any of them with ease. Second, David was confident he'd never break the rules of the house, which were that Daniel never touch them without supervision except in an emergency. He realized gun ownership came with some risk. But he was protective of the boy almost to a fault, and calculated those risks like a NASA scientist.

As Daniel returned the carton to the fridge, he said, "We bringing along the Ruger today?" The question was absent the hyper, impatient attitude of a typical teenager, cool-headed, just like his dad.

"Well . . . " David peered at the ceiling. "I guess we might could." He cut his eyes at Daniel and couldn't resist a half-grin. "That is, if you still want to."

The Ruger, a Mark III .22 pistol, had been Daniel's birthday present. The boy smiled and cocked his head, but remained silent.

Losing the staring contest, David chuckled and patted his son's shoulder. "Why don't I carry it, then we'll shoot it when we're done huntin'."

The boy nodded once and that was the end of it.

They were headed to Butcher's Gap, so named after Kevin Butcher, the settler who'd originally claimed the land. School started later this morning for most kids, but the Hayes family homeschooled. Daniel's teacher, his mother, still lay sleeping. Homeschooling freed them from the burden of public school scheduling. Daniel's mind was a supple sponge, hungry for knowledge. He was already working on senior year and even some college level material. They could afford to take this time together.

As far as anyone knew, the trip was for sport, the venison but a fringe benefit. But David's secret was that the food and hide would provide that much more they wouldn't need to buy with money they didn't have to spend.

They wordlessly segued into packing the Jeep, working as one, then left for Butcher's Gap, the sun still but a promise in the east.

≈ ≈

Thank God.

Devin James welcomed the hideous taillights as he would have the first glimpse of a sparkling tree on Christmas morning. He realized he'd been leaning forward in the seat, as if to extend by a few inches his view of the road ahead. He sat back and relaxed.

Tension seeped back into his bones. *Wait a minute.*

He instinctively reached for his cell phone, then remembered he didn't have it. He glanced at Jimmy's phone on the floorboard. No, it had offered the time on neither the dial pad nor the login page.

He scanned the dashboard. No clock.

He'd clicked off the music. He found the power button and punched it. Deafening gansta rap blasted the cab—but the display showed only a song title and time-lapse.

He clicked off the noise.

He supposed it didn't matter anyway; there was no telling what time he'd run out of gas, so he had no point of reference.

Okay, so how long had he spent hoofing it down the Old Conway Highway? His sense of time had been skewed; his memory offered only brilliant flashes of pain every time his left foot struck the pavement. But it had to have been somewhere between twenty and forty minutes. Then dealing with the Whitlocks must have taken . . . what? Ten minutes? Maybe twenty on the outside? So he'd been delayed at least thirty minutes, and possibly as long as sixty.

He'd caught up in no more than ten. How was that possible?

Then the blood drained from his face when he realized the taillight was back in place.

His breath caught in his throat. He floored the accelerator and leaned forward again.

He immediately backed off.

Trying to force the car over would be reckless. He imagined the jalopy rolling like a two-ton lathe, disintegrating each time it smashed into the pavement. Jessi in the trunk.

And if he *could* somehow stop them without a crash, a firefight would no doubt ensue. In either case, Jessi could be—probably would be—severely injured or killed. In fact, under threat, the Machine Man may quite conceivably waste her intentionally.

And let's face a cold hard fact, preacher: Her body might even now lay rotting in the woods, the Machine Man headed home, his business concluded. If that were the case, what good would it do risking his life to nail the freak?

Patience, Master Pastor.

He never uttered the title except to himself, and even then only in sarcasm:

Way to go, *Master Pastor.*

Nice try, *Master Pastor.*

Patience, *Master Pastor.*

He was no master. Unlike someone deserving of the title, patience was a problem for him. In fact, he found himself often on edge, his temper inexplicably at the boiling point.

An explanation for the problem eluded him as if it were hidden just the other side of a door deep in his mind. He sometimes reached for it like a boy for his nightmare closet, but he could never bring himself to touch it, much less peer in. This reluctance to twist the knob only angered him further.

Grace Owen had flung the door wide open, revealing the monster, his soul laid bare for the scrutiny of everyone present.

Candlelight made a fire-lake of the unfinished oak table, the surface aglow as if by luminescent boulders in the depths. A nice wine buzz facilitated the illusion and loosened Devin's lips as he gazed into the pool. "At times like these, I wonder how I could ever be angry."

"You're not angry."

He looked up at Grace, her eyes aflame in the candlelight.

"You're sad, Master Pastor."

He creased his brow. Mike and Vivian, also seated at the table, seemed to fade out of existence.

"When you're so sad it scares you, it comes out as mad."

He squinted at her, squirmed in his chair.

"It's none o' my business, but since you brought it up, I think what you're sad about is God."

He flicked his eyes at Vivian, then back to Grace.

"You long to find Him. So bad it hurts. Maybe since you was a boy, I don't know. But you tried so hard you even wound up a preacher. And so now you stand up there ever' Sunday, strengthening everybody else's faith, but it's you you're talkin' to."

He shook his head, almost imperceptibly.

"And hey—I don't mind. You always bring me closer to God, even though you only pretend to believe." She waited. "Even to yourself." She sat staring at him in the silence. "But don't you see?"

He couldn't seem to feel his hands.

"You don't believe in God, Master Pastor."

No. That wasn't true. It was just . . . he was struggling to figure it all out, that's all. No big deal. Nothing to get excited about. No problemo.

Then why are you so angry all the time?

Despite himself, he felt it boiling even now. He slammed down the lid, pinned it to the pot with all his weight.

Why did people believe in fairy tales? Not that God was a fairy tale. But He wasn't what people thought He was. This much Devin knew. The farmer prayed for rain, even as the baseball team prayed for dry weather. Didn't they see it? How did God decide whose request to grant? By whoever prayed first? Or whose faith was the strongest? Or was a decision even made at all? It seemed to Devin you'd do just as well flipping a coin. Because at the end of the day, by virtue of logic, somebody's prayer went unanswered. And who were we to pray for anything anyway when we lacked God's bird's-eye perspective?

It vexed him that people missed this.

Like Cindy Barker. A high school junior, she attended church every Sunday. Devin had heard she'd been struggling with her math finals. Grasping her hand in the post-service grip-n-grin line, he asked about it: "Studying hard for those finals, Cindy?"

"Well, I was."

Devin cocked his head, waiting for the punchline.

"I wasn't getting nowhere. It finally dawned on me I needed to just stop."

"You mean quit studying?" Their hands fell to their sides.

"I realized I didn't *need* to study."

He shook his head and squinted at her.

She took a patient breath, blew it back out. "If the Lord wants me to pass, I'll pass. If He don't, ain't no amount of studying gonna change that."

It just doesn't work that way! He resisted the urge to scream, to pull his hair out.

But maybe it *did* work that way, and his faith was just too weak to experience it himself.

Cindy spied a friend in the crowd— "See ya Master Pastor." —and scurried away. He gripped the next hand in line, then the next and the next, quoting by rote his usual *God bless you*s and *See ya next Sunday*s.

Cindy's parents wholeheartedly backed her strategy. In fact, they themselves had been praying for a car. They were very specific about it: *We asked the Lord for a brand-new Toyota Camry, teal, cloth seats, with a radio and them 'lectic windows. If the Lord wants us to have it, we'll wake up one day and there it'll be, gleamin' in the driveway!*

Aint' gonna happen. Of course, he never voiced it. Because who was he to burst their bubbles? Maybe Cindy *would* pass the exam. Maybe the family *would* somehow end up with a new car. In that case, if he revealed his skepticism, he'd look like a doubting Thomas. More likely, their prayers would never be answered, in which case his lack of faith would be blamed for God's refusal to come forth with their blessings.

They had to be missing it.

But what if *he* was the one missing it?

And what was he doing preaching when he couldn't come to a firm conclusion about whom—or what, exactly—God is? What was he doing preaching when, deep inside, as much as he'd hidden the notion from himself, he couldn't shake the feeling that God, like Devin himself, was nothing but a fraud.

He sat staring at Grace in the glow of the candlelight. She smiled back at him, her brown eyes somehow comforting, yet challenging him. Vivian and Mike just looked on.

Devin crossed his arms. "I wouldn't say I don't *believe* in God. It's just that, well, He isn't what people think He is. I mean, He's real, I guess, but—"

"You *guess?*" Grace smiled.

He shrugged. "Well, He doesn't answer prayers, for example. I mean, not literally."

"Give me an example—" Grace rubbed her hands together. "—of a prayer you'd like answered."

"Okay, fine." He uncrossed his arms and propped his hands on his thighs. "I'm sick of maintaining our stupid swimming pool."

"Good! Be specific now. Name one thing you hate about that pool. Somethin' you'd like God to do for you."

"Alright." He nodded once. "It's got a leak in it—which we can't afford to fix just now—and we can't let the water fall below the returns. That would burn out the pump." He shrugged. "Without the pump, it'll turn into a duck pond."

"Mm-hm."

"So I'm sick of having to top it off every night." The pot was coming back to boil. "I have to drag the hose out and screw it to the spigot. Usually at night after work so I can't see what I'm doing. I don't know why I never change into a swimsuit, because I always get soaked."

Grace nodded.

"Then I have to drag it across the lawn, inevitably breaking off a few plants in the process." He realized his hands were fisted. With some effort, he cracked them open.

"Okay." Her voice calmed him. "Alright." She looked around the table. "Let's all hold hands and bow our heads."

Devin felt like he was sitting in the corner wearing a dunce hat. He held Mike's hand in his left, Vivian's across the table in his right.

He looked back at Grace, then bowed his head and closed his eyes.

"Heavenly father—" Grace's voice lifted as she launched into prayer. "—First, we just want to give thanks."

As she rifled off a list of their blessings, Devin's left eye crept open. He scanned the table. Vivian and Mike were at peace, eyes closed as if they were sleeping. Grace's face glowed like a prophet.

He closed his eyes, feeling guilty for peeking.

" . . . and Lord, we come to you now with a humble request. We ask that on this very night, you would fill up Master Pastor's pool for him." She paused. "To-night, father—"

Devin looked up at her, this time not surreptitiously. "Grace."

"To-night—" She seemed not to have heard him. "—because Lord, this humble servant, this good man sittin' here, he doubts your power and your love for him."

"Grace." A little louder this time.

"He needs to *see* your mighty hand at work. He needs to know you're real, God. So if it ain't too much to ask—"

"Grace!"

She looked up at him. "Hmm?"

He sighed, exasperated. "I already set it up to-night. Before we came over. I mean, the pool. The hose is in it, filling it as we speak. So . . . "

"Ya see!" she said. "It's workin'!" She clasped her hands at her chest.

They all laughed out loud at her relentless faith and caprice—and at this contest of stubborn wills. Devin couldn't resist a pained chuckle himself. The woman was truly blessed in her blissfulness.

In the same event, she'd validated both their views on God. He longed to see it from her perspective, to be in awe of something miraculous, something bigger than man. He longed to believe in God, to believe in himself—hell, to believe in anything.

As he'd driven home that night, Vivian had taken his hand. "You're a real soldier of God, Devin." She chuffed. "Especially considering how hard you're working to find him."

He felt her look over at him.

"But you don't have to."

He turned and met her eyes.

"Because He's right in front of you."

They both stared out the windshield again.

She said, "Back in Jesus' day, they decided ahead of time what their new king ought to look like. So they didn't recognize Him when He got there. How could they? Their minds were made up." She sighed. "So they hung Him on a tree." She looked over at him again. "Can't you see you're doing the same thing?"

He shook his head once, kept his eyes on the road.

"You'll never find the god you're looking for, Devin. If you want to find Him, the *real* God, all you have to do is stop trying so hard."

He creased his brow.

"Let Him come to you."

She turned once more to the windshield.

A pasture eased by on their left; the faint fecund smell of manure wafted in.

He sat baffled in the silence. *Let Him come to me? What was that supposed to mean?*

As if answering his unvoiced question, she said, "*I am.* That's what He said. God just *is*, sweetie."

She was right about one thing: What he sought in a god was something of his own creation. And if he *created* God, then that, by definition, was *not* God. In the same way, his image of a martial arts master was also something of his own creation—and unattainable by any mortal man. But what was he supposed to do? This revelation explained his problem, but didn't solve it. In fact, he found himself even deeper in the woods, lost, with not a clue as to the way back home. He wished he didn't think so much. He wished he could just lose himself in bliss. Like Grace did.

Like Grace had.

What a waste.

The scream of the low-rider eased him back to the present. The icepack had melted; he tossed the wet 7-11 bag onto the floorboard.

Whatever God was—even the god of his own creation—hate was not a part of The Big Plan. But he felt it now, searing hot, dominating his thoughts. He could no more resist it than he could stop the sun from setting. For the Machine Man, hate burned white hot inside Devin James, the flames licking at his heart, consuming his soul.

How long had it been? He didn't know what time it was, but no doubt morning would be breaking soon.

Mark 9:17-24

"Teacher, I brought you my son, who is possessed by a spirit that has robbed him of speech. Whenever it seizes him, it throws him to the ground. He foams at the mouth, gnashes his teeth and becomes rigid. I asked your disciples to drive out the spirit, but they could not."

"O unbelieving generation," Jesus replied, "how long shall I stay with you? How long shall I put up with you? Bring the boy to me."

So they brought him. When the spirit saw Jesus, it immediately threw the boy into a convulsion. He fell to the ground and rolled around, foaming at the mouth.

Jesus asked the boy's father, "How long has he been like this?"

"From childhood," he answered. "It has often thrown him into fire or water to kill him. But if you can do anything, take pity on us and help us."

" 'If you can?' " asked Jesus. "Everything is possible for him who believes."

Immediately the boy's father exclaimed, "I do believe; just please—help me overcome my unbelief!"

Chapter 5

They're starting to make sense.

The dead ones.

They say what I expect them to say, but so do I now. I must have gone insane. Or died. Hand-in-hand, we dance in circles. I laugh with them; but I am not happy.

Their hands are cold and stiff.

I miss the voice, but what am I to do?

I need a little help. A blue sky. Sunshine.

I need a friend.

＝ ＝

Bud Lawson inspected himself in the mirror. Couldn't see much; the murky predawn light made a ghost of him. But he could tell his shirt looked sharp and that the creases in his pants was straight as a ruler's edge.

A glint of gold caught his eye. He plucked the badge off the dresser and pinned it to his shirt. He patted it with pride. The hand in the glass looked leathery, but that was just an effect of the shadows.

"You ain't wearin' your vest." A sleepy mumble.

Via the mirror, Bud smiled at the lump under the covers. "Now, what does a man o' steel need with Kevlar?"

"Put it on."

He stepped over to the bed and patted Bonnie's backside. "This is Morrilton, not New York City."

"What, air's thicker in Morrilton? Bullets move slow enough to dodge?" She still hadn't opened her eyes.

He bent and kissed her head. "Now see? It's just that kind of sarcasm been spicin' up our marriage the last forty years."

"If your shirt ain't full o' vest when I come in, that handful you stole through the blanket is all the spice you gettin' for the *next* forty years." She burrowed into the covers.

"Love you."

"Put on your vest."

Vest-free, Bud Lawson steered the cruiser out onto the road and headed to the Reeds'. The car seemed to know the way.

An insulated mug sat nestled in the cup holder. What was it about that coffee smell? Seemed like a old friend welcoming him to each new day, ensuring him it would be the same as the one before, and the one before that and the one before that.

He pulled up to the double-wide. Aglow in the headlight beams, Ted Reed stood waiting at the mailbox. His baby's face belied the age his receding hairline suggested.

Bud thumbed down the window as he rolled to a stop.

Ted practically leaned inside. "Shoulda seen the catfish I caught last night. Must have weighed forty pounds. See, what I done was, I cut me up some—"

"Go get on your vest."

Ted's shoulders fell. "The damn thing weighs more 'n that catfish!"

"I'll wait."

"Come on now, Sher'f. This is Morrilton. Not New York City."

"What, air's thicker in Morrilton? Bullets move slow enough to dodge?"

Ted shot his hip and scoffed.

"Vest." Bud rolled up the window and plucked up the mic. "Mornin', Holly."

The radio crackled. "Finally. I been tryin' to reach you since 4:30."

"Now see, that's why I keep my ringer off." Bud chuckled and lowered his gaze to his lap.

"Might have a situation, Sheriff."

"Whose cat's stuck up a tree this early?" He picked a piece of lint off his pant leg.

"Ricky Beckman?"

"I know him. He got a cat?"

"Called in. Said the weirdest thing."

After a beat, Bud sighed. He depressed the button again. "What'd he say?" Holly was a gossiper at heart, liked to have him tease the information out of her.

"Said, 'I cain't wake her up.' So I says, 'Cain't wake who up?' And he says, 'Couldn't find my feet.' That didn't make no sense, so I asked him where he was at."

Bud refused to bite this time. He just waited.

Holly said, "Well, he didn't tell me, but he did say who he couldn't wake up."

Nothing but static. Seconds passed. Bud pressed the button. "Holly . . . "

"'Ms. Hart,' he said. I says, 'Becca Hart?' And he says 'Cain't wake her up.' So I'z thinkin', must be something's wrong at the store."

"Don't he work over there?"

"Delivers fresh pastries ever' mornin'."

"When was this?"

"Called just a minute ago. Right before you checked in."

Ted Reed the Michelin Man jogged through the headlight beams. He opened his door and plopped into the seat.

"We're headed over." Bud hung up the handset.

"So what I done was, I caught me some bluegill yesterday afternoon—"

"Got us a little puzzle to solve down to the Piggly Wiggly."

"—then cut 'em up and threw them in m' honey-hole. You know, out in them weeds opposite the dock?"

"Probly nothing, but we best be on our toes just the same."

"Get a lot o' snags out there, but I catch a lot of fish, too."

Folks in Morrilton were hungry for incident, but nothing ever happened. Not really. A call about a bear would turn out to be a raccoon. Big fire was nothin' but boys sneakin' cigarettes out in a field. Hell, he understood. Wasn't nothing to do around here but sit 'n watch cars rust.

Or fish.

"But here's the secret. Instead of a treble hook, I took the glow-worm off my bass rig. Now, I know what you're thinkin'. Don't nobody use nothin' but trebles and stink for cat. But I'm tellin' ya—"

By way of bluegill and bass rigs, bobbers and bait, they made their way to Piggly Wiggly.

Bud steered into the lot. Took in the scene. Subconsciously, he registered Ted saying something about noodling and snapping turtles.

He reached over and clicked on the spotlight. Scrutinized the single SUV in the lot. Looked like Grace Owen's.

He moved the beam right. A gaping hole yawned where the front door should have been. Glass pellets like diamonds glittered on the pavement.

Ted gasped mid-sentence. "Aw, Sher'f!"

Bud picked up the mic as he eased the car around the building. "Grace Owen get a job at Piggly Wiggly?" In the back lot, a bakery truck sat backed into the loading dock.

"Not that I know of."

Across from it, an old Chevy sedan. Becca Hart's.

"We takin' a peek inside." Bud hung up the handset.

The dock door stood open. Light from inside threw a welcome mat on the concrete. A catfish might feel so welcomed when it discovered a bed of bluegill guts.

Bud put it in park and stepped out, eyes locked on the door.

From around the lightbar, Ted whispered, "Gun?"
"Out 'n up."

～ ～

Tim Loveless glanced at the rearview.

Shit. Still there. Looked like a UFO or something, floating on some kind of blue cloud. Headlights out of a acid dream.

Couldn't be a cop. Surely not. Of course, cops drove all kinds of undercover rides these days, not just them plain sedans that yelled *Johnny Law* at the top of their lungs. Nowadays they drove Transams, Camaros, Corvettes—hell, once he even seen a four-wheel-drive barreling down the freeway with blue lights flashin' on the dash. But the idea was to blend in, wasn't it? Surely they wouldn't go flyin' around in some kinda clown car lit up like a damn Christmas tree.

Yet he couldn't shake the feeling it was following him.

The turnoff was about a mile ahead. Didn't have no sign; you couldn't hardly see it unless you knew it was there. Hell, it wasn't even a road. He wondered if this piece of shit would get him far enough in to get good and hid.

That was the problem with hot rides. Had to take what you could get. You couldn't hardly steal a four-wheel drive, 'cause these ole boys looked after their babies. Kept 'em parked in back. Put alarms in them. Even if he could steal one, other mudders would gawk at him like dogs sniffin' each other's asses. That wouldn't work a'tall, no siree.

'Course, what you was drivin' was only part of the secret. Lot of it was the driver his self, and ole Tim Loveless knew what he was doing.

One more glance in the rearview, and he cut the wheel right.

The car bottomed out in the ditch then surged forward, springs complaining. A flash of light burst in his eyes— *"Fuckin' hell!"* —when his head struck the ceiling. Goddamn shoulda put on his seatbelt.

He thought for sure the jalopy was gonna to fall apart on him. But he couldn't slow down, no sir. Had to keep his momentum going. That was one the secrets to gettin' through this shit.

He risked a peek at the rearview.

The UFO shot past.

Uh-huh. Now that made since. Damn whigger-mobile. Some redneck kid wished he was black. He wondered why he hadn't heard any boom and hum comin' from it. Seemed like ever' one of 'em had the stereo hard-wired on full blast. Hell, they probably come from the factory like that.

Fighting the wheel, pounding the Buick for all it was worth, he called over his shoulder, "Hang on, Little Mary! We almost home!"

Ted fumbled at his side with all the grace of a kitten wrestling a ball of yarn. He pointed the 9 skyward. Shot a glance at Bud. "What about yores?"

"I'm hidin' behind you." He let Ted lead him to the door.

Inside, they took a cursory glance at the stock room as they approached the windowed swinging doors. Bud's eyes swept the store through the Plexiglas.

He pushed into the dairy department. "You check up front. I'll poke around back here." As a last thought, he said, "Get y' finger off the trigger."

As Ted stalked down the dog food isle, Bud turned left to the milk. Didn't they need a gallon? He wondered if Becca might sell him a jug while he was here. Store wouldn't open for another two hours, but he could just give her a five and let her keep the change.

He sighed as he looked over the selections. Used to, you just went and bought milk. Hell, there was a time you plucked it off your doorstep—after glancing up and down the street so as not to get caught in your skivvies. Now glowing before him sat all sorts of newfangled colorful cartons. Half-fat, low-fat, skim, lactose-free, half-and-half, soy milk, almond milk, rice milk, goat's milk . . . hell, looked like they didn't even offer the stuff that come out a cow's teat.

His radio crackled. "Forgot to tell you."

He instinctively reached for the walkie at his side, then remembered a mic was clipped to his shoulder. He resented even having to carry it. He longed for the good ole days when you didn't have to worry about gabbing, least not until you was sittin' in the cruiser.

He pressed the transmit button and leaned his head left. "Yeah?"

"Vivian James called in last night."

Static. His eyes fell shut and he sighed. "And?"

"Said Devin went out to the Piggly Wiggly."

He waited.

"For brownie mix."

Bud pursed his lips and drew a calming breath. "That's it?"

"Never made it home."

He creased his brow.

"She called again just now."

Instead of waiting, Bud finished for her. "And he still ain't come home."

"Right." The lightest shade of disappointment tinted her voice.

Real head-scratcher. Ricky Beckman talkin' like he'z drunk at five in the morning, front door busted out, the Owen's SUV out front—now the preacher out cattin' all night. Not like him. Not like him a'tall. Devin James was a—

"Freeze!" From up front. Then, *"Don't move. Don't you move!"*

Bud's heart skipped a beat.

"Sherrr'f!"

Wide-eyed, he stared toward the front, as if he were a man o' steel, as if his x-ray vision could melt away the countless shelves of goods, and his dread.

Jessi gasped, floating in the compartment like a kite with no string—then the floor stole a grunt from her when she slammed back down to earth. Her teeth clacked together and her ears rang.

The car rolled her right, then tossed her through the air to the left, slamming her mercilessly into the steel sidewalls.

A wreck. Her skin flashed icy-hot. She searched in vain for something to cling to.

The car steadied. It bounced and swayed but no longer gyrated like a boy shaking a grasshopper in a jar. She breathed a sigh of relief, a wad of felt bunched in each fist.

Her breath caught in her throat. Any country kid sleeping on the backseat knew what it meant when a turn changed the drone of the road to the crunching of gravel.

She scrambled into action.

Why didn't you finish the job, big dummy?

Searching for the screw.

You freed your arms—way to go—but you didn't even start on your legs!

She scuttled to the corner, set to scanning like she'd done before.

Then you just had to rest your eyes, didn't you? Just for a minute, you said.

Back and forth, row by row, she searched in vain, trying to balance the need for both speed and thoroughness.

A minute turned into . . . what? An hour? Maybe two? Stupid stupid stupid!

She froze. Shot a glance at the seat back.

The screw. Poked into the pressboard, right where she'd left it. *Big dummy.*

She plucked it free, struggled upright. Dug into the tape binding her ankles. Each breach of the surface offered a satisfying **pop.**

She winced when she nicked a shin.

Pop.

Of its own volition, her right hand shot out, just before the car sent her toppling again. In her hand, the screw. Now tumbling across the felt. Black on black. Tumble . . . tumble . . . gone.

She flipped to her tummy, scanning the scarlet coffin. Her breath was a bellows fanning flames of panic.

There! Pinned to the felt like a tiny tin soldier.

She snatched it up, rolled once more to her butt, head wedged against the trunk lid.

Three more pops and she had to catch herself from the other side. "Come. *On!*" This time she held fast to the screw.

Pop.

In her mind's eye, *Machine Man* in bold white letters on black.

Pop.

The Ken-Doll face.

Pop.

Bloody goatee.

Pop.

She winced again; warm wetness trickled down her calves. She rubbed her leg through the tape.

Pop.

Pop.

In the dark forest of her mind, his corpse-white hand.

Pop.

Reaching for her.

Pop.

Reaching to touch her.

Pop.

Pop.

No.

Pop.

 No way.

Pop.

She simply wouldn't allow it.

Pop.

Pop.

He'd have to kill her first.

≈ ≈

"Put it away, Ted." Bud Lawson had seen a body or two in his day, most times on a accident scene. The blood and gore hit you hard. 'Specially your first time. He'd lost his lunch when he lost his cherry, but never since.

"Look what he done." A whimper, a whine.

Ricky Beckman knelt rocking before Becca Hart. Her body. The kid hugged himself, smeared in red like some aboriginal shaman.

Bud said, "Now think a minute, Ted. Ricky ain't but seventeen. Just a boy. He look like he could do something like this?"

Ted creased his brow.

"And remember the door all busted out?" Soothing. Almost a whisper. Into the silence, he added, "And he called it in, didn't he?"

The stench hit you harder. Least it did with Bud. It was different depending on how much time had passed. He'd once worked a drowning down to the bogs. Body'd been there a while. Catfish and turtles had got at it real good. Smelled pretty much like what you'd expect.

"Put it on down now, Ted."

With fresh bodies, sometimes it didn't have no odor at all. Unless there was blood. Big ole bucket o' blood, now, that's got some tang to it. You kind of smelled it on your tongue, like you was nursing a mouthful o' wet pennies.

"Oh Jesus." Ted shuddered. "Look at all that blood."

Wasn't something you ever got used to; you just had to learn to deal with it.

Bud found himself at Ted's side, one hand on his shoulder, the other laid gently on the gun. "Just put it away." He applied a little pressure; the gun lowered.

"Look at all that fuckin' *blood.*" Ted's voice cracked. His face was white as a sun-bleached deer skull, slick as pond scum.

"Get on away from this, Ted. Go find some bottled water. Cold if they got it."

Ted looked at him, seemingly confused. "Right." He fumbled the gun into his holster and wandered away.

Bud turned to the nightmare on the floor. "What happened here, son?"

"Made a big ole mess, didn't I?" Amazingly, Ricky chuckled. But he didn't smile.

"What happened?"

"Tried to help her." Ricky's eyes fell to the body. "Slipped in the . . . in all her . . . " A shudder racked him. He looked back up at Bud. "Busted my ass, Sheriff. Couldn't hardly find my feet." He shook his head and stared out at nothing.

Smears on the tile looked like the aftermath of a mud wrestling contest in a slaughterhouse. Or a finger-painting by God Himself, a macabre revelation of things to come, of the Morrilton that once was but would never be again.

"Who done this, Ricky?"

"Couldn't wake her up."

Bud just nodded.

This was Morrilton, not New York city. Him and Ted *was* the backup.

He thumbed the mic. "Holly?"

"What's goin' on over there, Sheriff?"

"Call over to Grace's. I expect you won't reach her, but let me know either way."

"This early?"

"And patch me through to the state police."

━ ━

Emerald Beams of sunlight trumpeted through the trees, some gilded gold by the first leaves of fall. Like angels heralding the new day to come, they seemed to promise peace, but nevertheless proclaimed God's dominion, be it peace He bring or otherwise. In the heart of Devin James, both love and resentment stirred, and fear and peace, comfort and dread.

The taillights brightened. The jalopy slowed. His heart kicked at his chest, demanding action. All he could offer was a light pump of the brakes.

He peered in the rearview, hoping to discover another motorist on the road. He didn't even bother praying for a police cruiser.

Nothing but sun-speckled blacktop back there—and of course trees—and trees and more trees, miles and miles of trees.

He instinctively reached for the blinker—then snatched his hand away. *Why don't you just flash your lights and lay on the horn while you're at it, Mister Master 007?* He shook his head at his almost-screwup.

In fact, he realized, he shouldn't even follow them in right away. He'd end up right on top of them.

He rode the brakes, gently, trying not to be too obvious about it.

The Buick cut right, plummeted into the ditch, then leapt back up the other side and plowed into the underbrush.

Devin maintained his speed, taking in all he could of the logging road, if that's what it was, and how the car was doing navigating it. Pretty much what he'd expected—a pair of slanted taillights disappearing into the trees.

He focused once more on the highway.

Now what?

Well, maybe he'd run across some help. He hadn't seen another vehicle for hours. But the sun was up, so maybe some farmers were, too.

He floored it, praying he'd run across a slow-moving tractor, a hay truck—perhaps hunters entering the woods.

Nothing.

His eyes turned to dinner plates.

What if they'd just been turning around?

The Buick had looked pretty committed, plowing into the woods like it had. But still. What if, tired from the drive, Machine Man had missed his turn? Devin scanned his memory for any hint of a road—a sign, a mailbox—anything. He recalled only endless blacktop. But then, he himself had been grainy-eyed, too.

In his mind's eye, the Buick pulled back out onto the highway then rocketed the opposite direction.

He stood on the brakes. Blue smoke roiled around the car to a shriek as if from a pterodactyl.

He executed a slick u-turn, amazed at how well the low-rider handled the maneuver. Under different circumstances, this may have been fun.

He punched it again, peeling slabs of rubber, and steered out of a screaming fishtail. The tires caught purchase and he barreled back the way he'd come.

After half a minute, he began to worry. *Where's the turnoff?* He slowed, desperately scanning the roadside. "Oh no," he muttered. "No, no, no . . . "

There!

He cut the car hard left.

The front bumper dug into the ditch then sprang back up, heaving earth and sod like a manic shovel-loader.

Rocks and dirt clods rained on the roof.

Something slammed into the undercarriage. Deafening. He was immediately assaulted by the pungency of motor oil spiced with a hint of gasoline.

"Shit shit *shit!*" The little car was hell on wheels on blacktop. Off-road, however, he might as well have been riding a bobsled.

He swerved left, then right, spinning the wheel, slipping and sliding, trying desperately to keep it on the trail—or even to *find* the trail.

A branch slapped the windshield. Weeds and saplings raked the paint job, nails on a chalkboard.

Glass shattered beneath the car. The blue cloud had glowed its last.

The engine suddenly screamed, though the car lurched to a stop. In the side view mirror, the left rear tire was a potter's wheel, a good foot off the ground. It slung mud for a beat—then nothing but air. He didn't even bother trying to maneuver it free.

He killed the engine. Kicked open the door and hopped out. Three steps into a sprint, he stumbled to a stop. Cut back to the car.

He leaned inside, punched open the glovebox.

Vehicle manual.

Pencil.

Lighter.

Bag of weed.

He shook his head and slammed the box shut. He peered over the seatback, scanning the seat and floorboard, for a spare magazine, another pistol, knife, water . . . maybe a cell phone if he got lucky.

Nothing but a crumpled Taco Bell wrapper.

Backing out, he considered the cooler. Amazingly, it still sat upright in the passenger's seat. About an inch of water pooled in the bottom. He snatched it up and stood. Turned up the cooler, corner to his mouth. He drank greedily.

He tossed the cooler, already marching into the weeds. Plucked the 9 from his waistband. Extracted the magazine. Two rounds, as expected. He slammed it back in the well.

He dodged a tree, leaped over a puddle.

He eased back the slide, spied a gleam of brass, let it snap back into place. Stuffed the gun in his pants.

He bolted into the woods.

━ ━

Loveless found a wide place in the trail and worked the car to face back the way he'd come. Wasn't much chance he'd have to hightail it, but you just never knew.

Like ole Coach Tanner used to say, *Ain't no harm prayin' for sunshine, boys, but always brang a raincoat.*

He killed the lights and cut the ignition. Statue still, he stared out the windshield. The pinging of the engine lulled him.

Though only a mutter, his voice shattered the silence. "Please, God."

Knobby knees . . . scrapes and bruises.

"Let it be her."

Sweet little freckles.

"Please?"

Ponytail bobbing, shimmering, the very source of the sunlight.

He glanced at the back seat in the rearview. "Is it you?" He strained his ear for an answer, knowing it would never come. "Are you The One?"

After an eternity, he rolled down his window and scanned the woods. Listening. Only birds and squirrels out there, raising their usual daybreak ruckus.

He couldn't hardly believe they'd finally made it. Seemed like they'd *never* get here. He realized his gut was all knotted up like it used to get before a tough game. He closed his eyes and breathed in the sweet morning air. Calmed his self.

He sighed and twisted the rearview to face him. Inspecting his mug. After a few adjustments to his hair, he slipped on his D-shades and plucked his overcoat off the seat.

He unfolded from the car. Took another scan of the woods as he situated his coat. Doggone it, his ole hands was shakin' so bad he couldn't hardly get it on.

He straightened the lapels. Shot his cuffs. Fine tuned his shades. He had to look his best, wanted everything to be just so.

He rolled his shoulders and cracked his neck. As a last thought, he brushed off his t-shirt.

He found himself at the trunk. After staring down at it for half a minute, he said, "Now, I'm just as scared as you, Little Mary." He shuffled through the ring to the trunk key. "Hell, I cain't hardly hold the keys steady." Sure enough, they trembled before the slot, jingling. He chuckled, immediately sobered himself, then cleared his throat.

He jammed in the key. Turned it.

The trunk lid whined slowly open.

Tim Loveless gasped. He couldn't believe what he was seeing. His heart soared; his knees turned to rubber.

She knelt before him like a handmaiden.

His chin quivered and he blinked back tears.

She faced not toward him, but to his right, as if not to presume to face him directly.

Doggone it, how did she always know just what to do? His whole life, she'd made him feel like he *was* somebody, and now, by God, she was makin' him feel like a damn royal prince. Hell, a king!

But that was enough; she'd won his heart. She was his, but he was hers, too.

It was time he showed her. "Hey now—" He bent to stroke her hair. "—you ain't gotta . . . "

His hand froze. His brow beetled.

What happened to the packing tape?

BAM!

Flash of light. Brilliant on the right side. *Way* brighter.

The rocky ground spun up to greet him. Hit him. *Smash!* Bashed into him like a damn Mack truck. He grunted; his teeth rattled in his skull.

As he slowly rolled to his back, arm floppin' like a dead snake, his mind started a instant replay of what just happened.

She come springin' up like a damn jack-in-the-box. He saw it now, looping over and over before his mind's eye: Spring, *SLAM!* Spring, *SLAM!*

She'd hit him with something. Something *hard.* What was it?

"Tryyy Roarrrn," he muttered, then wondered what the fuck he just said.

Oh.

Tire iron.

She'd fixed herself sideways not out of respect, but so she'd be wound up like Goddamn Babe Ruth. Ready to knock his ass out the park. She'd swiveled her whole body, backhanded the shit out of him with the iron.

"Niiice," he said—then wondered who'd said it.

His eyes rolled; fuzzy leaves danced on a stage of blue.

Birds and squirrels.

And ringing, like the TV tone when a station went off the air.

Birds and squirrels.

And now something bigger. And something warm trickling into his right ear. He winced at another flash of pain.

Birds and . . .

Wait. Something bigger? Yes. Something *way* bigger 'n a damn squirrel. A deer? Yeah, had to be a deer.

Ain't no deer, dumbshit. That there's Lil' Mary, just a shittin'-and-a-gittin' it through the Goddamn underbrush.

He bolted upright, hands braced behind him. Fought off a wave of nausea. A flash teased at his eyes. Little piece of glass or something on the ground, shootin' a beam of sunlight back at him. He shaded his eyes, leaned to examine it. "Aw *hell* no!"

Bitch done smashed his D-shades. Glass all busted, frames bent to fuck like a mess o' Goddamn metal pubes.

More crashing from the underbrush. Waaay back there.

And fadin' fast.

While he sat here on his ass poutin' about his damn D-shades.

He struggled to his feet. Stumbled across the road. He leaped into the briars and went stomping after the little shit.

━ ━

Run! Run! Run! Run!

Her heart was pounding at her throat.

Run to where?

A branch lashed her face.

Doesn't matter. Just keep running. Just keep running.

Briars like razor wire.

Kids get lost in the woods all the time.

Spiderweb! Too late. Plow right through it.

So do it on purpose. Just get lost.
Plucking sticky strands from her face, her hair.
What about food and water?
Something tickling her neck. Run!
Find a stream. A pond. A lake.
Something big.
Berries and crayfish.
Smack. Smeared on her palm, brown slime swirled in green and yellow—
Where would you sleep?
—and legs like hairs still kicking.
Doesn't matter. Run. RUN!
Something struck her ankle. Tripped her up. She went sprawling into a patch of vines.
Soft landing. Good.
Or *not* so good.
Bird in a snare. Can't get up. Nothing to grab. Can't get up. *Can't get up!*
"Come 'ere!" His grip was a leg iron, welded to chain. He dragged her roughly from the vines.
Roll like an alligator!
That little stunt cost her a shoe. But it worked.
She wormed. Belly-crawled. All-fours. *Run!*
He snatched the other leg from beneath her. She body-checked the earth.
Breath gone. Shooting stars. Ringing in her skull.
She tried in vain to roll again. Death grip: Kneeling, he had her in *both* hands.
She shrieked.
He dragged her close, closer, close enough to—

She slammed her heel into his face. Once, twice; when he freed a hand to block his face, she yanked the pinned leg free.

There goes the other shoe.

Just go!

She belly-crawled into the briars. Bare feet plowing stony ground. Elbows rotten tomatoes with nerves. Thorns entangle silken strands, rip them out in frays.

He latched onto her ankle again. She kicked and struggled, wormed and kicked.

His grip slipped; he snared her pant leg.

"NoooOOO!"

He dragged her free of the vines once more. *Lifted* her.

She found herself squirming like a snake by its tail, staring at his upside-down belt buckle. She looked up at the ground.

A stick like a doe roller. She groped for it. Quivering fingers stretched to capacity.

Just out of reach. Agonizing.

He fished for the other pant leg, hooked it. Chuckling.

She squirmed and struggled harder still.

He faltered.

She snatched up the stick. Slammed it in his crotch.

He roared. "Stop! *Hurting me!*" His boot lashed out. Rapped her skull.

She dropped the stick, dazed. Swinging limp now.

He stomped his boot onto her hair. Lifted again.

Her pants were sliding down. Up. Off.

She fumbled for her belt. Not wearing one. She grasped two loops instead, then fistfuls of pant rim.

Fire in her scalp. Tears spilling into her eyebrows.

"Stop! Kicking!" Gravel in his throat.

She froze, death grip on the pants, panting. Biceps trembling.

Voice as if from an oil drum: "If you *calm* down, I'll *set* you down."

Oh yeah, and then what?

Her pants slipped another micro-inch. Arms quivering. Fingers like Play-Doh. Blood-filled face like a blushing boil.

Slipping . . . Slipping . . .

He'll have to kill me first.

She released the pants, sacrificed them like a lizard giving up a tail.

Machine Man teetered, stumbled, fell. The pants flew over his head.

She rolled, reeled, ran.

Tripped.

Huh?

Panties bunched around her ankles. She pedaled, pushed, kicked and prodded. One leg free.

GO!

Ariel, Sebastian, Flounder and Prince, swept and brushed and broomed the earth. Little Mermaid panties swinging wildly on one ankle.

She found an opening in the vines. Ran right in. Points like needles. Lashing her legs. Spines like fishhooks. Stinging her feet.

Punch like a hammer into her spine, he grasped her shirt. Flung her like a rag doll back into the clearing.

Stunned, she rolled onto her back.

The ground was cold. *Too* cold.

Where's my shirt?

The world dimmed.

She peered up.

Silhouetted by the sun, he was a shadow. In his hand, a shadow shirt.

Torn to rags.

She flopped to her belly, floundered for the briars.

No wonder bunnies like the briars.

She squirmed and wiggled, wedged and scooted, snaking into the vines . . .

And he caught her ankle again. Skin on bare skin, his hand was a python.

No more shoes to lose. No more pants or shirt to shed, she was a lizard, fresh out of tail.

He'll have to kill me first.

She dug her fingers into the earth. Flexed with all her might.

He yanked. Ten furrows in the ground.

He yanked again. "Get out here!"

She spied a spindly scrub oak sapling.

Yank!

She released the earth, snared the tree. Nails caked with dirt and blood.

"God*damn* it!" *(Yank)*

The sapling held.

"Let go!" He tugged again; her shoulders were exploding.

"Let!" *(Yank)* "Go!"

Pebbles rolled away from the tree. *(Oh Please God no.)*

Tug!

A little earth gave way.

Yank!

A little more.

He grabbed both ankles, tugged with all his might.

And the root ball broke free.

She slid for miles over roots and twigs and shards of stone. Bare belly. Skin in bloody shreds. Stubbornly clinging to the sapling trunk.

She crossed her legs. Flipped to her back. Crunched her abs. Brought the tree around like a baseball bat . . .

Mom? Mom? Mom?

"Mom?"

She gasped. *Who said that?* Heart slamming in her throat.

She whipped her head left. Then right. Slowly scanned the woods.

Twittering in the trees, caprice cardinals capered. Cicadas sang. A bee buzzing somewhere.

Her eyes fell to the ground. She gasped again.

Machine Man. Groaning. Face like roadkill, caked with mud, pebbles, blood. The uprooted sapling by his head, a hard-packed-dirt-mace on a stick. He bent his knee, dragged one boot slowly through the leaves. Groaned again.

She found herself flying, pounding the earth, leaves lashing out like Kamikaze killer bees.

Run! Run! Run! Run!

＝ ＝

The headlights were glass eyes, the Buick a steel gargoyle seemingly standing vigil for him through the trees. Squatting, he tested several angles, leaned left and right, lowered and raised his head. He eased aside a branch—carefully, quietly—tried still more angles.

Devin cursed inwardly, unable to determine if they were over there. He let the branch ease back into place.

He studied the woods to his left, then his right.

Left. That way seemed the most passable, or at least less *im*passable.

One eye always on the car, he navigated the underbrush, bent like a hunchback. It was as if the gargoyle car had laid a minefield of sticks and twigs, dead limbs and leaves, each set with a hair trigger to broadcast his location by a betraying crunch. He felt like a contestant in a Twister game from hell.

After what seemed like hours, he finally located a spot that revealed the Buick in profile through a foliage tunnel. Even absent the glass-eyed stare, he found the gargoyle illusion no less disturbing. It seemed as if it only pretended not to see him, like it might suddenly lunge, snapping teeth of twisted steel the moment he was within reach.

The trunk was open.

Hard as he strained to hear them, no muted voices disturbed the stillness. Only birds and squirrels playing in the branches, heard but not seen except in fleeting glimpses. He almost checked the gun again but decided he was only delaying the inevitable.

He snapped the pistol to a two-hand grip, letting it lead him from his hiding place, charging the car, not running but with measured haste. He blew each quick breath out through pursed lips.

At the car. Finger on the trigger. Blow away the freak, pull up for Jessi.

No one in the passenger's seat—nor the driver's, nor the back.

Rustling leaves behind him.

He turned, gasped, squeezed the trigger. A hair's breadth from firing.

Only a turtle. That's what he told himself. Or a rat or a rabbit or maybe a fox. A shiver traversed his spine, converged in his scalp. He followed the sites of the pistol as he turned, slowly, a full 360. Scanning the woods.

Have to check the trunk.

I don't want to check the trunk.

Have to check the trunk.

Still scanning the woods, past the point at which he'd started, he thought about why she might be in there.

Unattended.

With the lid open.

Then he stopped thinking about it.

Have to check the trunk.

Just to be safe, he slid his back along the car, muzzle skyward, edging toward the back—then burst around the corner and jammed the pistol into the compartment.

He turned and bent, propped his hands on his knees. Gasping for breath. He didn't know whether to be relieved or agonized Jessi wasn't here. Considering what he might have discovered in the trunk, he chose relieved.

He stood. Hustled to the passenger's door. It opened without resistance. He leaned inside, scanning the interior as he had the Toyota's.

Nothing.

He popped the glove box; the door plummeted like a dislocated jaw and spilled the contents onto the floor: A tube of lipstick. A glass angel. What must have been a thousand crumpled Kleenex, some bearing rose-colored kisses.

A church bulletin.

What the . . .

He teased it out, careful to avoid the Kleenex.

Jameson Baptist Church. Interesting.

He used the rolled bulletin to brush away the tissues, scanning the other items.

Tire pressure gauge on a keychain. Tiny cross on a gossamer golden chain. Several cough drops, the medicine long since fused to the wrappers.

Vehicle Registration.

He snatched it up: *Tinsey Tillman.*

Ah. That explained the inexplicable choice in vehicles. Maybe Tinsey was his mother, or maybe he'd stolen the car. Regardless, he locked *Tinsey Tillman, Jameson* in memory.

He backed out, circled the car, scanning the rock-and-weed road. A glint caught his eye. He hurried over, stooped to investigate.

The Smokey and the Bandit shades. Mangled. He cocked his head, squinting.

He kept searching. At the far side of the road, hiding in the weeds, a tire iron. The bend in the tool appeared gummy. Maybe grease or oil.

He bent to retrieve it.

Not grease. Not oil.

His gaze wandered to the crushed glasses. A single chuckle escaped him. "Way to go, kid." He was surprised to hear a tremor in his voice.

He dropped the tool and tiptoed gingerly into the foliage, careful to disturb as little as possible. Preserving the scene. Seeking. Searching.

He knelt to a pine seedling pressed into the mud, studied it like a haruspex sifting through innards.

He scanned farther out.

A broken stick.

Of course, sticks could be broken by deer, a fox, falling branches—or anything at all. So was this evidence of passage or just his imagination?

He gasped. Stood. His heart was a panicked herd, hooves on asphalt. He pushed through the underbrush.

He stopped. Stared. Studied.

Tangled in a hanging vine, strands of blond.

Jessi stood frozen, naked and afraid—yet enchanted—eyes locked with the deer's. A doe, perhaps a mother, it seemed to mirror her feelings.

Each assessed the other, considering their options.

Jessi broke the silence. "Mama?" Her voice shook, and her body.

The deer's flanks quivered, perhaps ready to bound into the woods. Surprisingly, Jessi felt a tinge of regret at the thought.

The deer wiggled an ear. Its eyes seemed to calm.

Perhaps Jessi's nakedness had some disarming effect, or perhaps instinct told it they were both victims on this day, members of the same sad sorority of the hunted.

The doe pawed the earth, lowered its head and huffed a cloud of mist. It turned, picking its way through the underbrush. After a few steps, it looked back and blinked. Waiting.

Jessi followed.

They picked their way through briars and brambles, the deer sometimes skittish but nevertheless matching Jessi's slower pace.

They broke into a clearing. Just ahead, a steep rocky hill of maybe twenty feet. The deer deftly made its way up the rise, rocks tumbling away in its wake. It stopped abruptly at the peak. Stood statue still.

Four hooves suddenly stomped, startled. Jessi jumped with the deer. The doe crouched, a coiled spring.

Chills racked Jessi's spine. Gentle or not, wild animals were unpredictable. Horse strong and lightning fast, a deer could kill you. Absent antlers, it was nevertheless equipped with sharp hooves, powerful legs.

The doe stared down at Jessi. It seemed to strain for the power of speech, as if yearning to tell her something important.

Still mute, it turned and leaped into the briars—and out of her life forever.

She topped the summit where the deer had stood. Smeared in mud, streaked with blood, she was a little-girl Jesus headed for the cross. But like Jesus, her spirit remained unbroken, clean and whole, her dignity intact.

She stood unashamed and defiant on the peak of the hill.

Down the other side, maybe thirty yards away, a man with a mustache slowly lowered a rifle. Staring up at her.

A teenage boy stood behind and to the side of him. They both wore orange camo and, even from this distance, she could see they had unusually large ears.

＝ ＝

Sadness crushed him, and a sense of overwhelming loss.

Betrayal. Treachery. Deception. How could she do him like this?

Loveless trampled a sapling, pummeled his way through a briar patch. Cursing under his breath.

Fuck that. He was no sissy; he wasn't sad.

Just pissed.

He broke a limb thick as a man's wrist with one stomp. Slapped aside a low-hanging branch.

His damn eyes was on fire. Drainin'. Not tears, just blood and what felt like battery acid. Couldn't hardly see out the right one. Overcoat pricked to fuck, pants heavy with cockleburs. The backs of his hands was sliced to hell, burning and itching. Bleeding. And he'd stepped in deer shit.

He snatched up a stick like a baseball bat. Laid into a briar patch, beet-faced, teeth gritted. "Take *that* you little bitch!" He swung again. "And *that!* And *that!* And *that!*"

His way cleared, he spun like a discus thrower and heaved the stick into the woods.

On second thought, he wasn't just pissed. He was hot as the fires o' hell. *Seething* mad. No more Romeo. No more Mister Nice Guy. He was going to find this little shit, scalp her damn ponytail and plant his boot up her ass.

He realized he was chanting in time with his steps: *You ain't her. You ain't her. You ain't her.* He denied hearing the slightest tremor in his voice.

A clearing.

Finally.

He bent to rest, hands on his knees. A little hill with a fairly steep rise bordered the clearing. Panting, he considered the hill. Hell, maybe he'd be able to scout the terrain from up there.

He wrestled his way up, a trickle of dirt and pebbles in his wake.

He topped the hill.

Froze in his tracks.

"Well fuuuuck me." Just a mutter, under his breath.

Right down the other side, not thirty yards away, stood his Little Mary. He'd have marched straight down there, except for two things.

First, she was holding a canteen. The canteen weren't no problem, 'cept it likely belonged to the big-eared, skinny little redneck in orange camo pants and flannel shirt knelt down on one knee like he was Goddamn proposing to her.

Little Mary was wearing his jacket. That or she found a damn Walmart hid way out here in the brush somewhere and bought it with a fistful of squirrel shit n' oak leaves.

The second problem was a little more worrisome. Another redneck, about twice the size of the first, sporting the same orange camo and even bigger ears, stood staring back at him, complete with high powered rifle and a mustache like Goddamn Burt Reynolds.

Now, he could draw his ole .45 and start slingin' lead. That idea appealed to him. Problem was, at this distance, he might as well o' been slinging paper airplanes. And by the looks of that scope, ole Redneck Reynolds would be able to pick out which one of Tim's buttons he wanted to poke a hole through.

He'd have to play this smart-like. Run a little deception play.

For that to work, he had to believe it himself.

Tim Loveless *became* Mary's father, all tied up in knots, worried sick about his little girl. He patched together a quick history—the day she'z born, her chores around the house, her favorite supper (catfish, of course), and what he got her for Christmas last year. "Mary? Mary, honey?" He stumbled blindly down the hill, eyes locked on the girl. He stopped for a beat, just for effect, then hustled forward at a brisk walk. "Oh my God."

He steepled his hands. "Oh thank you, Jesus."

Twenty-five yards.

His pulse picked up. Not from nerves, no sir. Because he was so relieved to find his girl! Good. He was believin' his own bullshit. "She ain't right in the head, you know."

Twenty yards.

He weighted his eyes with worry. "Mary, baby, what're you doin' runnin' around out here butt naked?" He chuckled and shook his head.

Fifteen yards, and he thought he could push it a little farther.

"Cain't take your eyes off her even for a second." He jogged two steps, then resumed his pace.

Ten yards.

"Where'd ya'll find her?" He thumbed open his overcoat. Nice and easy.

Seven yards.

From seven yards, it'd be *him* deciding which button to punch through their damn guts.

He eased his hand toward the piece. He could almost *feel* that ole checked grip nestled in his palm.

Redneck Reynolds raised the rifle. *Clack-ack!* "That's close enough, mister."

= =

Wasn't nothing like the sound of a rifle rackin'. Stopped a man cold in his tracks, oh yes it did. Like runnin' smack into a damn brick wall.

Tim slowly raised his hands.

By the looks of the muzzle, Mustache was totin' a thirty-aught-six. Maybe a three-O-eight. Either round would eviscerate his ass, knock down the tree behind him and kill a damn cow a mile away before it even realized it'd left the barrel.

His throat bobbed.

Something trickled down his face. Right out his damn eye. Blood, no doubt. Goddamn it, that's why it hadn't worked. His ole face probably looked like he just stumbled off the set of *The Walking Dead,* gagging and hissing and hungry for flesh. "Hey now." He shook his head once. "I know this looks—"

"Tell it to the judge. Sheriff's on the way." Ole Redneck Reynolds' mustache twitched, up high on the left side.

Nerves, most likely. Hell, he was probably scared shitless. It was hard, pointing a gun at a man. Even harder shootin' one. For most folks. Tim smiled inwardly, bided his time.

"I reckon you better hand over that Colt."

He eased his right hand to the .45. Maybe this was gonna be easier than expected.

Ole Mustache raised his voice— "Left hand pinchin' the handle." —and twisted his hands on the rifle.

Goddamn it. Tim raised his right hand, pulled out the piece with his left.

"Now toss it on over here."

He did like he was told. Nice and easy. "Hey now listen, fellas—"

"I don't wanna shoot you mister, but by God I'll do it." Then to his boy, "Son, neutralize that weapon, if you please."

"Yes sir."

Yes sir. Like he worshiped the man. They'z rich, no doubt. Tim scoffed inwardly, almost shook his head in disgust. He hated that about rich people. Always puttin' on airs. *Yes sir no sir. My daddy gimme this. My mama kept the kids last night.* Like they was a damn happy-ass squirrels' club or something.

The boy locked eyes with him as he stepped forward. Tim resisted the urge to jump and holler, *boo!*

The kid ejected the clip, then racked the round out the chamber. Tim Loveless looked on like a tiger might watch a baby through the bars of a cage. The boy stuffed the piece in one cargo pocket, the ammo in the other.

Ole Redneck Reynolds smiled. Though he tried to hide it, it was clear he was right proud of his boy. *What for?* Hell, anybody could clear a damn gun.

Rich people.

"This little girl's told us some ugly stuff here. State police backs her story."

Shit. How the hell'd they find out so soon?

"If there's some kind of mix up, you can straighten it out with them. But I ain't taking any chances."

Tim opened his mouth to speak.

Mustache raised the rifle. "Best just get on your knees."

Tim knelt.

"Hands on your head."

He smirked, sighed, did as he was told.

Hands laced on his damn gourd, he shifted his eyes to Mary. She was shivering. Little punk put a arm around her. She tucked her hands to her chest and nuzzled up to him. "I'm cold."

Now ole Tim's upper lip quivered. Not out o' jealousy, no sir. Just disgust at how rich people always stuck together, that's all. Shoulda knowed she'z rich, with them fancy pants. And when he seen her mama didn't carry no purse. Probly pockets full o' credit cards.

"How are your feet?" Redneck Reynolds. "Up for a little hike?" He spoke to Mary, but never let his eyes stray from Tim. Smart of the old bastard.

"Yes sir. I'll be fine."

See? Rich.

Mustache nodded. "Take her on down to the Jeep, Daniel."

Tim locked the name in memory.

"Use the spare key. Get her some water, maybe a bite to eat out the cooler."

Tim cut his eyes from one of them to the other. Lettin' them split up wasn't no good a'tall.

"Cut on the heater and fetch her a blanket."

If he'z gonna make a move, he better make it soon.

"Yes sir." Lil' Daniel boy escorted the girl like she'z a cripple. Or the queen o' damn Sheeba. The boy was skinny as a skeleton. Tim's ole .45 looked like a boulder bouncin' around in his pocket.

They was right by a little valley, he realized. Hell, he hadn't even seen it up to now. Couldn't tell how steep or deep it was; but the other side rose up maybe 100 yards away.

The kids faded over the edge.

⸻

"Oh no." Devin laced his fingers in his hair. "No no no no no." He approached the little shoe, but only stood staring at it, as if picking it up might make it real. It seemed to burn his eyes somehow.

He blinked.

He looked away, only to discover a shredded shirt—filthy, spotted with blood.

And jeans adorned with embroidered butterflies.

He trembled. A mewl escaped him. He turned in circles, taking it all in, until dizziness made him stumble.

He propped his hands on his knees. Shook his head. He squeezed his eyes shut, fighting off nausea. On the backs of his eyelids, sepia tone images of what had happened here. Or was happening elsewhere even now.

Stuck.

The woods were a blind maze. Only by wild chance had he found this place. Every step he took in further search could just as easily lead him farther away.

What he'd found here assured him she was dead. Or worse.

His eyes snapped open. He stood. His anger shoved the nausea aside. "Okay, why?" He spoke only to a congregation of trees.

"Why?" Arms extended, listening, he genuinely wanted to know.

"I offered you my *life,* but that wasn't good enough. No, you prefer to see *her* stuffed in a trunk all night. To send *her* through hell. Does that make you feel good, Old Man? *Huh?* You just sit up there on your celestial ass and look on while she loses her mother. Her *mother!* And you haven't the decency to take me instead? Even when I *offered?"*

He scoffed. "Why is that, exactly? Is it *me?* Is that it? I'm not faithful enough for you? Well in case you haven't noticed, I've been trying *real hard* with you! I mean, it's really pretty stupid when you think about it, because, *I don't even believe you exist!"*

It was the first time he'd said it out loud. Although the words shocked him, the confession felt good.

"Yet I dedicate my life to *trying* to believe in you. *I'm a preacher* for Christ's sake!" He laughed deliriously. "What kind of damned sense does that make?" His voice cracked. "Talk about your faithful servants."

He spit on the ground. "I do everything just like you say." He lowered his voice mockingly. "Oh, we gotta always *give thanks* first." He paused for effect, staring up at nothing. "Even in tough times, we *have* to thank the *Big Cheese,* because He takes care of us.

"But you know what? You don't."

At the top of his lungs, he repeated, *"You don't!"*

He paced, fuming, then made a decision.

"I'm done." He scanned the earth, plucked up a fist-sized stone. With a few steps for momentum, he chucked it at the sky. "I'm sick of you!" The rock soared. "I'm finished!"

His chest heaved.

"You hear me? *Finished!"*

Devin watched the stone rise—then inevitably descend, slowly, twirling, crashing through the foliage then landing with a thud, having fallen well short of its target. The echo of his voice died in the woods.

No lightning struck him.

No trumpets sounded.

No bushes burned.

Only the birds answered his angry prayer.

The years caught up to him, and the night. He collapsed to his knees. His shoulders shook.

Grace Owen: Dead.

Becca Hart: Dead.

Jessi: Dead or dying.

He was powerless to save them, powerless to help.

Powerless.

He'd tried so hard—throughout the night for Jessi and throughout his life with God. He didn't know what to say, what to *do.* Life, it seemed, had led him to this miserable end.

Lost.

His tears subsided. He shook his head. There was a slim chance Jessi was still alive out there. And maybe if he got *really* lucky, untouched.

God was not going to save her.

It would have to be him.

But where else could he look? What else could he do? Tromping blindly through the woods may take him closer—but may lead him farther away. Hell, he could easily get lost in Butcher's Gap and end up needing rescuing himself.

Face it.

Defeat.

His only hope was God.

Like a child crawling back to his mother after yelling, *I hate you,* Devin turned his face to the sky. "Okay." He nodded. "Okay, you win." He shrugged. "I'm sorry; I'm finished." He lowered his head. "I hope you can forgive me."

He was probably just talking to the trees right now, but he continued. "I offer myself to you, *again,* just like I always have. I'm here, even though you never have been."

He gasped.

He'd once read somewhere that schizophrenics lack the normal neurophysiological function of corollary discharge, by which people and animals are able to distinguish between external auditory sounds and their own internally generated thoughts and speech. In other words, the voices they heard in their heads were their own.

In the serenity of the wilderness, *his* voice echoed in his mind, as if they'd been spoken by someone else:

I offer myself to you, again, just like I always have. I'm still here—even though you never have been.

Devin James sat perfectly still.

Birds twittered in the trees. A chorus of leaves whispered secrets on the breeze.

He got it. After all this time, he finally *understood.*

God Is.

Hidden in plain sight, glorious in its simplicity. He'd been searching for something complicated. Elusive.

Forbidden.

But God had always been there.

And always would be.

God was right here, right now. He was part of Devin, or rather Devin was a part of Him.

God *does* have hands.

Our hands.

God would not bless Cindy Barker with an A in math just because she prayed. But He had, already, provided her a mind with which she could *study.*

And perhaps God would bless her family with a new Camry—if they put to use the spine with which God blessed them and worked their asses off to earn it.

Or not, and that would be okay, too.

But only when we've done our due diligence, prayerfully, to make it happen ourselves will God's will truly be known.

God *does* answer prayers.

Sometimes the answer is *No.*

And only when we've spent our lives genuinely searching will God reveal Himself to us, as He was to Devin right now.

How had he missed it? He had neither the burden nor the ability to create God.

He created *us*. He *is* us. He is reality itself; He is everything.

God just Is.

As a matter of fact, in the same way, Devin didn't have to—or get to—proclaim himself a master. Or *not* a master. Or a white belt or black belt or any rank at all. That decision was solely on his instructor. Devin could still work hard, he could still fight—but he didn't have to worry anymore. And that meant . . .

He was free.

Effortless effort.
Hurry up while standing still.
Do it, but let God do it.

It was time to shut up and stop trying to control everything. It was time to let go and let God.

Just. Let. Go!

He sat for a moment, eyebrows knitted.

When worry crept back into his heart (*Run! Search! Panic!*), the urge to redouble his efforts tempted him.

He resisted it.

That was his old self talking, trying to reassert control, trying to do everything himself.

Instead, he thought of Psalms 27:14: *Wait on the LORD: Be of good courage, and He shall strengthen thine heart: Wait, I say, on the LORD.*

His hands were God's hands.

He closed his eyes and prayed. "You just tell me what, when, and how, Old Man. I'll do it." After a pause, he added:

"I surrender."

— —

New Testament Apocrypha, Gospel of Thomas:

Jesus said: "If your leaders say to you 'Look! The Kingdom is in the heavens!' Then the birds will be there before you are. If they say that the Kingdom is in the sea, then the fish will be there before you are. Rather, the Kingdom is within you and it is outside of you.

Split wood, I am there. Lift up a rock, you will find me there."

Chapter 6

Back where I started. Is it tomorrow? Yesterday? No time here . . .

The voice led me back—but did she guide my travels or just remind me I'd never left? It's frustrating, this lack of control.

It's good to be home, if you could call this home. But nothing's changed.

Stalemate.

She seems to love me, but she asks of me something I cannot give.

I can't. I won't.

"No! You hear me?" I ball my fists at my sides. "Stop trying to convince me!"

She just prattles on, her voice echoing about the cavern.

Then she sings to me.

Despite myself, I close my eyes and listen.

Perhaps today I will not try at all.

Just listen.

He wasn't going to no prison, no sir. Machine Man, he'z a big ole boy, but he'd be no match for a gang of rock-ribbed Nancies.

He was no sissy. Wasn't nobody's fuck doll.

Gonna have to make another little withdrawal from the truth bank.

See, the secret to lying was telling the truth. 'At's right. People learned to trust you. Hell, you needed to believe your own damn self if you wanted to pull off a good one.

Take catfishin'. Ole Tim'd dump him a big ole bucket of chicken innards out to the pond, just about ever' week. Then he'd stand there talking to them fish like a damn fool. Real friendly-like. And he really felt it, too. Cared about the little critters.

Then one night when one them chicken livers turned out to have a hook in it, why ole Mister Whiskers wouldn't even know what hit him.

Like ole coach Tanner used to say, *Always tell the truth, boys. 'Cause you never know when you gonna need a good lie.*

"I need to tell you somethin'." He found Jesus, oh yes he did, right here, right now, right out in the middle of the woods.

Ole Mustache didn't even so much as bat a eye.

Tim nodded. "I'm a piece o' shit." His voice broke. Deep in his heart, he felt it, truly believed in his soul he was a broken man. He realized his chin was quivering. *Damn* he was good at this.

Mustache said, "This ain't no confessional, and I ain't a priest, now."

Tim watched him real close, without *lookin'* like he was watching. Ole Redneck Reynolds tried to hide it, but he was feelin' some pity for him. Just a little bit. Oh yes he was.

In his peripheral, the kids just startin' up the other side of the damn valley. Better pick up the pace.

"There's somethin' else."

Mustache seemed to be done talkin'.

Tim sighed. "There's some*one* else. Out here with me."

There! Yep, he seen it, oh yes he had. Ole Reynolds' mustache ticked again. Up high on the left side, just like he expected. Ever' man had a tell, and ole Burt's might as well have been a pair o' damn high-beam headlights.

"Chester. His name's Chester." He shook his head once. "We split up to find the girl." He felt like a damn sot on Sundie mornin', confessing his Saturday night sins to God 'n everybody. *Tell it all, brother!* "I don't know what he'll do if he finds us here, but I sure know what'll happen if he runs into them kids."

Old Mister Mustache was just a hoppin' and a jumpin' all over Big Burt's face.

"Chester likes boys." He shrugged. "I like little girls, okay?" His voice broke. "Like I said, I'm a piece of shit." His vision clouded and his voice wavered. "I only got eyes for my Little Mary. But Chester, he likes boys." His head fell to his chest and he worked up a sob.

Mustache took his hand off the grip.

Watch him now, watch him!

Circled his fingers at his lips.

Not yet . . . Not yet . . .

He looked out over the valley, let loose a big ole whistle. "Hey Dan—"

Damn he loved football. Ole coach Tanner had worked him hard. Made him bull strong. Lightnin' fast.

Smart, too.

He knelt before ole Redneck Reynolds, right up agin' him. Fist balled against the man's chest like he was pleadin' for something.

The rifle had gone off. Blasted a damn duck pond in the dirt. Hell, he'd hardly noticed. He realized he was clenching the barrel in his left fist.

He stayed froze like that, just a second or two longer, just to be sure. His hands was a pair o' damn table vices. Hell, his arms was shakin'.

He smiled up at Mustache. Mustache was starin' back down at him. Confused, he was.

Tim sprang up— "Gimme that!" —and snatched away the rifle. Ole Redneck Reynolds' eyebrows was a bumpin' and a grindin' like a couple o' caterpillars trying to fuck.

"N' use common sense! You don't *never* take your eye off a prisoner, or your hand off the gun that's holding him!"

Hell, he wasn't listening. That's okay, that's alright. Ole Tim understood. He lowered his tone, slowed down a little. "That feelin' you got?" So Burt could understand. "That's shock." He let that sink in a minute. "And that handle stickin' out your chest, that's a old ax handle. Used to play with it as a boy.

The ax handle, I mean. Wanted to keep it around after I outgrew it—" He pointed at the handle. "—so I sawed it off and made me a knife out of it. Keep it in my boot."

Ole Mustache took a look at it. Seemed like he couldn't hardly believe it was there.

"Seven inch blade on it. Nice, huh?"

Redneck Reynolds collapsed to his knees. And damn if he didn't *still* look confused.

"I'z aiming for your throat, but you backed up a little on me. Lucked out gettin' it between your ribs."

Reynolds' eyes wandered out across the valley. He was white as a damn sheet, swayin' like a willow in the breeze.

"I ain't no doctor, but I reckon I nicked y' heart."

Big Burt looked back up at him.

"It's pulsing. See?" He pointed at the wound.

Reynolds looked down at it. Took holt the handle with one hand, held his chest with the other. Blood just a globbin' out over his fingers like red toothpaste.

"Might last a little longer if you leave it be."

Ole Burt looked up at him again. Under the mustache, his lips was blue.

"Blade's got it plugged up, see. If you *pull* it out, you gone *bleed* out." He shrugged. "But I'll leave that up to you." He examined the rifle again, a little closer now since he didn't need to worry about Mustache no more. "By the way, this here's Chester." He looked back at Mustache with a big ole shit-eatin' grin. "*Win*-chester! Git it?" He racked the bolt. "And he do like boys."

A gunshot split the morning.

Devin's eyes darted up, scanned the woods.

He found himself standing. He was no expert, but he knew the difference between the reports of a handgun and a hunting rifle.

Just a hunter?

Maybe. Probably.

But maybe someone had run across them. Seen Machine Man for what he was. Shot at him. Maybe with luck, the bullet had found its mark. At the very least, this meant the arrival of help.

His heart soared. *Thank you, God. Oh thank you for this.*

Of course, he couldn't just walk up on a hunter without announcing his presence. That would be a little tricky since the shooter may turn out to have been Machine Man. After all, while he knew the freak was carrying a .45, he couldn't be sure he had *only* a .45.

The shot had come from maybe fifty yards southwest.

He checked the magazine and breech, yet again, just to be sure.

As he started forward, a question crossed his mind, as it always had at moments like this: *God or dumb luck?*

But the answer this time—as it would be from this day forward—was simply, *Yes.*

Pistol in a death grip, moving as quickly as he could, as quietly as he could, he followed the report.

Jessi flinched at the boom of the rifle. Dropped reflexively to her tummy. She spun her head around and shot a glance across the valley.

Machine Man was kneeling before Mr. Hayes. It looked like he was proposing. Or pleading for something.

Machine Man stood. Jerked the rifle away.

Mr. Hayes dropped to his knees. Jessi's breath caught in her throat.

She found herself scrambling up the hill on all-fours. Though she hadn't made the decision to ape-walk on purpose, it seemed to work better for navigating the slope.

Daniel . . .

She stopped, snapped her head around.

He stood frozen in place, staring across the valley. "Dad?" His voice cracked. Then yelling—*screaming:* *"Daddy?!"*

"Daniel." There was nothing they could do for him. *"Daniel!"* She remembered the Piggly Wiggly parking lot, how she'd been cast in concrete, cemented to the pavement. No force on earth—no words, no reasoning, no clap of thunder—could have broken her free.

She sighed and hobbled quickly back down the hill. She looked up at Daniel, then across the valley. Then back to Daniel. "There's nothing we can do for him." She grasped his sleeve. "Come on." Tugged at it. "Daniel, come *on!"* Yanking and pulling and pleading.

He refused to budge.

Through the scope, Loveless watched the boy reaching out toward him from across the valley. Lil' Mary was just a tuggin' and a yankin' on his sleeve.

He was holding a Weatherby Vanguard Sporter .308 hunting rifle, accurate up to five hundred yards— even beyond that if the shooter knew what he was do- ing. 8x scope on it. He could just about make out the zits on the boy's face. "What you got this sited in at, hundred yards?" He shifted the scope to the girl. "Hell, they just standin' there. Dumbasses."

Mustache husked something. Loveless lowered the rifle and looked down at him. "What'd you say?"

"Please."

"Hell, I might o' got caught a lung, too. Or ye windpipe. Cain't hardly hear you."

"Please."

"Huh? What?" He put his hand to his ear.

"Please . . . "

"Hell, I'm just playin'." He chuckled. "Now, help me pick out who gets to go first." He peered back through the scope, shifted from one little shit to the other. He muttered, "I truly cannot decide."

"Can't breathe."

He lowered the rifle again and looked at Mustache. "Yep, that's what I figured. Better calm down. Ever' time y' heart beats, why it's filling that ole lung up with blood. Suffocatin' ain't no way to go."

Tim gasped— "I know!" —then raised the rifle again: "Eeny. Meeny. Miny. Moe." He shifted the muzzle on each beat. "Catcha. Redneck. By-tha. Toe."

"Daniel!" Louder this time. Louder husk anyway.

"What's 'at? The boy first?" Old man was reaching out across the valley. Like that'd do him any good.

"Daniel." Still just a husk.

Tim's eyes lit up. "Why, that there's some smart thinkin'! Lil' Mary, she's barefoot, ain't she? Cain't run as fast."

"No. *Please . . . "*

"Uh-uh now. No take-backs." He laid the cross-hairs dead center of the boy's forehead. Slowly squeezed the trigger.

Right as the rifle boomed, Goddamn Mustache grabbed his boot.

⸺ ⸺

Zzzip! The ground exploded just behind them, fol-lowed immediately by the report. Jessi ducked reflex-ively and squeezed her eyes shut. Echoes of the blast cascaded through the hills.

She turned to Daniel. He was gawking back at her. She screamed, "Let's *go!"*

He nodded, faltered—then shot up the hillside.

Jessi took off after him.

⸺ ⸺

"Goddamn it, look what you done!" He glared at Redneck Reynolds. "You ruint my concentration!"

Loveless shook his head and took a giant step sideways. Racked the rifle again. Checked on ole Mustache one more time.

"Please . . . "

That did it, Goddamn it. Tim snarled and put on a whiny tone. *"Please please please! No no no! Daniel Daniel Daniel!"* He spit on the ground. "Rich sissy." He raised the Weatherby. Peered through the scope. Squeezed the trigger. That ole rifle kicked his shoulder and drilled his damn ears out. Best feelin' in the world.

Boy's head exploded like a watermelon.

He lowered the rifle. *"D'you see that?"* He whooped with delight. "Got him at a dead run! *Right* in the damn head!"

Redneck Reynolds was circlin' the drain. Looked like he got rode hard and put up wet. He muttered, "I love you, boy," just a starin' out across that valley. His eyes seemed like they'z made out o' glass.

Tim slowly shook his head, staring down at ole Mustache. "That is some seriously fucked up, faggoty-ass shit."

Old man didn't hear him. Hell, he'z already dead.

≈ ≈

Alone at last. Just the two of them. *Finally.* Loveless found the orange camo in the 8x scope.

Spilling down the jacket like melted gold, her ponytail.

Shimmering.

The very source of the morning sunlight.

His pulse kicked up. His ole breath come in fits and starts.

He swallowed hard. Started shakin'.

He lowered the rifle. "Is it you?" His lips kept moving, but he couldn't hardly hear what he was sayin'. His breath hitched. His throat bobbed.

When his vision clouded, he gritted his teeth and snarled. "Aw *hell* no." He racked the bolt.

Buddy o' his got him a d-vorce a while back.

He lifted the rifle.

Said somethin' made Tim laugh his ass off.

He found the orange camo and quoted his friend: "No matter how hot she is, no matter how cool she seems—" Locked them cross hairs right dead center. "—somebody, somewhere, is sick of her *shit.*"

He squeezed the trigger, nice and slow, hungry for that ole kick. "Fuck your damn ponytail. You ain't her."

——

Just as he came to an incline, a second report froze Devin in his tracks.

In one way or the other, a deer would be a ghost after the first shot. Only rarely would a hunter get a second.

Unless they were hunting something else.

The bottom dropped out of his stomach.

The third report was a cattle prod, sent him scrambling up the slope. From over the peak, whoops of laughter.

Quickly. *Quiet!* Slipping. Tripping. The hill was a down escalator littered with marbles.

He reached the summit. His hands grew heavy and his spine turned cold. The freak spoke casually to a downed man, to a lump in orange camo. Utterly unmoving.

Devin's eyes traversed the valley.

Another lump. Also unmoving. Crown of scarlet chunks and bulges.

His heart hammered. Heaved. Hopped into his throat. He shook his head, trying to convince himself it was a dream.

Just a nightmare.

So wake up.

Wake up.

Wake up!

The freak raised the rifle.

Across the valley, scrambling up the hill, a third figure. Bare legs of ivory, ribboned in red. An orange camo jacket five sizes too big.

Blond ponytail.

He almost called out but choked it off. He'd do nothing but make a target of himself. By the looks of that scope, the freak would not miss.

Take a shot at him?

At this distance, he'd do as well chucking a spear.

He hustled down the hill on legs like stilts, quietly as he could, certain the freak would turn any second.

Machine Man lowered the rifle. Seemed to mutter to himself.

Devin picked up the pace. Hopping, skipping, scanning for bare ground free of twigs. Mind on overdrive.

Twenty-five yards.

The freak raised the rifle again.

Now. Now! *Shoot him now!* In his mind, the pistol boomed. Target down. Done. Dead.

He didn't do it. Still too far.

Patience, Master Pastor. The freak would need a moment to center the shot.

He scrambled, scooted, leaped and skipped. Almost fell. Caught himself. Still silent.

Twenty yards.

Still too far.

No choice. No time.

He raised the pistol. Two-hand grip. Slowed to a crab walk.

Breathe.

He stopped and braced, a statue, an anchor, a sword in a stone.

Effortless effort.

Centered the sites.

Hurry up while standing still.

Centered his mind.

Do it, but let God do it.

His trigger finger flexed.

Take your time!

Make it count.

(Patience, Master Pastor.)

Somewhere in the wilderness, a mother jay screamed in despair.

— —

Ba-Bam!

Funny feeling come over him outta nowhere. He felt dizzy. Hell, drunk.

Tim Loveless shook his head, trying to clear the cobwebs.

Big ole tuft of lining come poppin' out that orange camo. He was sure of it. But then he pulled right. Lost sight of her. How come he done that? He *always* followed through, kept the sites locked in after the shot. That was one the secrets to hittin' the target. Follow-through.

He stretched his eyes wide open. Gazin' at the damn grass. Tried to blink his mind clear.

The rifle had misfired; that's what it was.

No, not a misfire. Not exactly.

It fired *twice*.

He creased his brow, flabbergasted. Examined the bolt.

Bolt weren't no problem. Splash o' blood like a red boutonniere on his bicep was a *big* damn problem.

What the hell?

Something slithered in his stomach. Fear cloyed to panic.

He snapped his head left.

Rage consumed him, numbed the pain. *"Goddamn it!"* Words come poppin' out his mouth before he even

realized he said them. "What is this, a damn *commu-
nity gatherin'?!*" He racked the bolt. "Cain't I get just
one!" Raised the rifle. "Second!" Fixed the cross hairs
on the numb-nuts. "Of *privacy?*"

He squeezed the trigger.

— —

The pistol cracked and the rifle boomed. Devin's
heart tripped. *Which shot came first?* He thought he'd
hit him, but couldn't be sure. Even if he had, had he
been too slow? Late by a millisecond?

Which shot came first?

He looked across the valley.

Jessi was down. Still as a corpse. *Oh God . . .
Please, God, no.*

He blindly lowered the pistol, owl-eyed. His heart
was a jackhammer, pounding at his chest.

She seemed to stir . . . then shot scrambling up the
slope. Devin breathed a sigh of relief.

"Goddamn it!"

His eyes snapped back to Machine Man.

"What is this, a damn *social gatherin'?!*"

The racking of the bolt seemed to rattle Devin's
spine. He raised the 9.

"Cain't I get just one!"

What if I miss?

"Second!"

Machine Man wouldn't.

"Of *privacy?!*"

Devin dove right.

Something punched her to the ground. Seemingly pinned her there.

Heat. Like she was clamping a curling iron under her right arm.

Jessi struggled to her elbows.

Smoke curled out from a hole in the ground, just beneath her shoulder. Like a crater left by a buried firecracker.

Tufts of fine floating feathers caught her eye, wafting around her like falling snow.

The curling iron became a fire poker. White hot.

She winced. Eased her left hand beneath the jacket. Blindly examined the burn. She sucked a hiss through her teeth when she ran across a channel in her flesh as if laid by a pencil in Play-Doh.

Warm wetness. She didn't need to examine her fingers to know what it was, but she did it anyway.

Her hand trembled. Smeared with scarlet. Her breath was a hand rasp, filing down her hope.

She scrambled up the hill.

Goddamn it, ole numb-nuts was slicker 'n a damn alley cat covered in Crisco. Dove *right* out the scope, right when he had him nailed. Didn't hit nothing but a oak sapling.

Machine Man lowered the rifle. Little fucker was laying there littered with wood chips like a damn Calvin Clean model been working a chainsaw. Drew a chuckle outta Tim.

Then with a crackle like a grizzly blazin' a trail, that ole tree come a falling. Right toward numb-nuts.

"Timberrrr!" Tim yelled. His chuckle turned to a belly laugh. Why, this just kept gettin' better and better.

Ole numb-nuts rolled to safety, just as the tree bounced to the forest floor. Slicker 'n owl shit, oh yes he was. Had to give him that. Little shit turned on a dime and raised his gun. 'Cept there *weren't* no gun!

Tim laughed even harder, slapped his knee. "Missin' something?"

Little fucker went to peepin' and a peerin', just a swattin' and a battin' them branches. Looked like a cat chasing a laser dot.

Tim racked the rifle. Raised it up.

Little Man got real still. Looked up at him through the scope. Started talkin' to his self—

"Boy, you oughta see the *look* on your face!"

—or maybe prayin'.

Like that'd do him any damn good now.

Machine Man squeezed the trigger.

　　　　　　　　＝＝

Devin hit the ground like a sack of rocks. His teeth rattled in his skull. Crackling, splitting, splintering. In his head?

"Timberrrr!"

Movement caught his eye from above. He looked up to find an SUV-sized canopy whizzing toward him.

He bunched his body, shoved off, rolled free.

He stood. Pivoted. Brought up the piece.

The freak howled in laughter, slapped his knee. *"Missing somethin'?"*

Shit.

He desperately scanned the ground, the maze of limbs and leaves.

There! Barricaded by branches. He dug in, clawing desperately for the 9.

Just out of reach. Agonizing.

Machine Man racked the rifle.

Devin slowly stood. *Checkmate.* "Guess this is it, huh?" Under his breath, but not to himself. "It was a good run, Old Man." He straightened his shoulders. "Thank you for my life. For Vivian, for Jessi, for Grace and Mike." Funny, he felt no fear.

"Boy, you oughta see the look *on your face!"*

"Guess I'll see you in a minute."

━ ━

The Weatherby Vanguard Sporter .308 hunting rifle has a maximum capacity of six rounds: five in the internal mag and one in the breech. While engaging the safety might offer some protection against accidental discharge, how easy would it be to trip the switch inadvertently?

David Hayes was a cautious man. Responsible to a fault. He'd never have carried a gun with a round in the breech, especially with Daniel in tow.

≃ ≃

Snap!

Firing pin on an empty breech. Sweetest sound he'd ever heard. *God or dumb luck?*

Devin smiled.

He leaned into the limbs and snared the Glock, amazed at how easy it seemed when he wasn't in a hurry. He navigated his way around the fallen tree, watching Machine Man puzzle at the rifle. "Missing something?"

The freak looked up, eyes wide with panic. He racked the bolt. Fired from his hip.

Snap!

"Boy, you ought to see *look* on your face." Devin couldn't resist a grin as he closed the distance. "Set it down." He raised the 9.

Machine Man just stared at him, flummoxed, then gazed at the rifle again.

"Set it down," Devin repeated. "On your knees."

The Winchester clattered to the ground. Machine Man knelt and placed his hands on his head.

Devin arrived in front of him, considering his options. The man's face was a horror show. So was his soul, but it was not Devin's place to judge. "Before today, you'd have been dead by now."

Machine Man nodded. Stared at Devin's shoes. "I'm a piece of shit." His chin began to quiver.

"Worse than that, I'd say."

"I deserve to die." His voice cracked.

"Yes, you do. But that's not my call."

The freak looked up. Blood had flooded the outside of his left iris. "There's something else."

"There's nothing else."

"I mean, there's some*one* else. Out there." He jutted his chin at the forest. "We split up to find the girl, see. I don't know what he'll do if he finds us here, but I sure know what'll happen if he—"

"Don't bullshit me. Just sit there and shut up, you lucky son of a bitch."

The Ken Doll corpse face turned to stone. "What'd you call me?"

"You called yourself a piece of shit. I thought you were being generous."

"No. Just now!" He seemed suddenly furious— "What'd you call my *mama?*" —like his rage outweighed the threat Devin posed.

Psychotic was bad. Reckless was worse. "You need to calm down and—"

Machine Man exploded. So *fast!* One hand clamped down on Devin's wrist, the other on his throat. A stockade of flesh and bone. Mask of hate.

Devin found himself clawing at the noose at his neck. Exactly what he *shouldn't* do. His attention riveted to his airway, to the fireworks blasting behind his eyes, he failed to maintain a firm grip on the gun.

Machine Man shook his wrist like a pit bull. The Glock flew free. Devin's vision closed to a pinhole, blinded by the light show.

Calm down.

Can't calm down!

Think.

Can't think!

Calm down and think, or die.

He ducked. Bobbed left. Broke the choke. But his wrist was still clamped as if to a wall of granite.

He twisted his wrist, shot it down. Simple as pie. Just like he taught in class.

Except it *didn't* go down. Wouldn't budge. Sometimes with kids, they needed two hands.

He parried a punch, stumbled a step, grasped his right fist in his left. Ducked under the freak's arm.

His wrist broke free at last.

He scanned the ground. *Where's the 9?* (Exactly what he *shouldn't* do.)

A fist like an anvil slammed his head. He ducked. *(Huh?)* Another punch sailed over him. He retreated a step. *(Never back up!)* He stopped in his tracks. Ducked and turned. Spun and kicked. *Hard.*

Machine Man grunted, didn't go down. Now he was laughing.

Laughing!

Devin kicked again. Right in the gut. He might as well have kicked a bull.

A bull with hands, the freak snared his ankle.

Devin leaped. Hooked with his heel. Satisfying thud. His ankle broke free; the ground came up to greet him.

Machine Man teetered. Tripped and fell over the lump in orange camo.

Devin rose on his elbows. The freak was staring back at him over the corpse.

Painfully obvious, right between them, the handle.

Closer to Machine Man.

The freak grinned.

Devin spun to all-fours. Fanning the leaves. Flailing. Sweeping. *Where's the pistol?*

The freak chuckled.

Devin risked a glance back.

Machine Man was going for something else. Not the knife. He flipped the camo jacket back. Snared a checked grip. Drew out a pistol.

He found himself raking. Swiping. Flailing.

Machine Man: *"Scrub that floor, little man!"*

Where's the pistol? *Where's the pistol!*

Shoo-clack! Raucous laughter now.

There! A good five feet away. Damn.

Devin sprang up.

(Crack!)

Launched.

(Crack!)

Flew.

(Crack!)

Tucked. Snared the 9. Rolled. *(Crack!)* Lead bees flying around him. *(Crack!)* Some close *(Crack!)*, some closer. *(Crack!)*

He landed. Pivoted. Spun as he stood. Squeezed. *No!* Lock in the sites. *(Patience, Master Pastor.)*

Boom!

Machine Man twirled, seemingly *threw* the .22 as if it were a Frisbee. He stumbled, toppled. Curled into himself. Writhing.

A sudden sense of calm washed over Devin. He started toward the freak.

Curiously relaxed.

Euphoric. *Everything's going to be A-Okay.*

Machine Man shot a glance at him, started crabbing for the .22. When his right elbow struck the ground, he shrieked in pain. Dropped his head. Then kept crabbing. He was a tough one; had to give him that.

Devin pinned Machine Man's ankle with his foot. When the freak kept struggling, he bore his weight down on it.

Machine Man dropped his face to the ground. Bellowed in rage at the dirt. Gasping for breath.

"You done?" Devin's words seemed to come from somewhere in a dream.

The freak sighed and rolled slowly to his back. He pressed his left hand to his right upper chest. Blood oozed out between his sausage fingers.

Devin kept the 9 trained on his face. Trigger partially depressed. He would no longer make of himself an easy foil.

After a beat, the freak smiled. Then chuckled.

Despite himself, Devin smiled back. "What?" He felt like he'd been nursing a beer. More like a whiskey bottle.

"Reckon I caught y' liver."

"What?"

"Blood's thick. Dark." He pointed at Devin's belly. "See?"

— —

Pain blossomed like a black rose bud. Funny how he'd felt fine—great, in fact—until he saw the dark sludge oozing from his gut. Devin pressed his hand to the wound, just under the right side of his ribcage. He grimaced. Groaned. Snarling.

"Ain't nothin' but a .22, but a liver shot, that'll put a man down."

Devin stared back at Machine Man. The freak faded and resolved. Rippling.

"Oh yes it will. 'Specially if they'z hollow points."

Devin stared out at the woods, then up at the sky.

"Got about a hour, maybe more. Less if you move around alot." Machine Man winked. "Like say, walkin' outta here?"

Devin batted his eyes, pursed his lips. A bolt of pain shot up his spine.

"Say. Ain't you the one I killed back in Morrilton?"

"Tried." Devin grunted again.

"God*damn!* You got nine lives, boy. Who are you, anyway? Cop or something?"

Devin turned his gaze to the east. The little figure, orange camo jacket five sizes too big, gazed back at him from across the valley. Silhouetted, she was dazzling in the morning sunlight. She scampered down the hill, headed this way.

Devin smiled. Turned back to Machine Man. "I'm Master Pastor."

"Pastor?" The freak chuckled. "Well hell then! You cain't kill me!"

"Yeah, and why's that?" Devin tightened his grip on the 9.

"You a man o' the *cloth!"* The freak flipped to his belly and scrambled for the .22.

Devin shot him in the back of the head.

He lowered the spent Glock. Let it slip from his hand. "You know, I've actually been kind of working on that."

━ ━

Tim Loveless thought he must be dreaming.

He was floating, light as a feather, naked as the day he was born. Entranced, he took in the passing Spanish moss.

No, not moss. His ponytail forest. Only bigger. *Much* more dense.

And beautiful.

He smiled, stroking the manes as he passed.

Shuffling drew his attention. Hard-sole shoes on tile. He wondered how this could be, for there was no floor. Nor were there walls or ceiling. Only brilliant light, seemingly from all around him.

He strained his eyes to see through the hair, shifted left, then right. He caught only fleeting glimpses— buckled shoes, the hem of a skirt.

The steps again. Seemingly searching.

The footfalls ceased—then changed direction.

Mary?

Mary!

He realized where he was. How had he gotten here? No matter; *she* was here.

His Mary.

His Mary.

That's all that counted.

"Over here!" He laughed ecstatically. "It's me! Timmy!"

The shuffling stopped—then turned straight for him.

He held out his arms, trembling with anticipation. "Mary." A whimper. His chin quivered.

The floating hair wavered, swelled in the approaching draft.

Closer . . . closer.

Timmy creased his brow. "Oh no." The light curdled to murk.

Even before he saw, he knew.

He *knew*.

He shook with dread, then bellowed in terror. But he couldn't seem to move.

Gentle Ben now a spiked splintered tabletop, it ripped away scalps, sliced the air. Clearing a path for the New and Improved Big Bitch Battle Ax. Her skull was an exploded watermelon.

Putrid green, lined in yellow.

Spattered with red.

Squirming with maggots.

"BEND OVER!"

Chapter 7

I sketch a lioness on the drawing wall. Mom's humming from the den comforts me. She's folding laundry.

The humming draws near; she rounds the corner to the kitchen. I look up from my work. Our eyes meet.

And I remember.

Primal scream. Two shots like thunder.

My smile fades and my pulse quickens. We're in a dream—but not a dream.

A visit.

"Mama?" My voice cracks.

"Oh, honey." She shakes her head, eases toward me. She's got that typical Mom look on her face, like everything's okay, like communing with the dead is, while kind of sad, really no big deal.

But she loves me; that much is clear.

My chin quivers as the distance closes.

She hugs the folded sheets to her tummy like a school girl sometimes carries her books. I open my arms. Close my eyes. Dryer-warmed laundry presses my face—so fresh and clean . . .

She walks right through me.

The laundry falls to a heap on the floor. I turn, but she is not there.

Now here—Nowhere.

≈ ≈

That was twenty years ago—the first of three visits my mother paid to free me from the cavern.

By way of my dreams.

It was the first time I'd faced her death.

But there was much work to do.

Each visitation brought a new revelation. The second was similar to the first.

≈ ≈

I folded the small stuff, socks and things. Mom handled the larger items, sheets and towels. We chatted happily as we worked, blissfully unaware of the tragedy that cursed us in the waking world. In this vision, it was her *mom who'd died.*

She sighed as the conversation lagged. "Ah, Jess, I need to move on with life." She plopped a towel on the stack. "But I can't! Nothing's real or makes any sense. Nothin' tastes or smells or feels anymore." She shook her head. "If I could just bury my mother."

This was very unlike her. Grace Owen didn't pout, even about death.

I was happy to be the one to play counselor this time. "I miss her too, Mom. But I know she was your mother, so she was extra-special to you. But I also know—and you do too—that she loved you like crazy." I looked up at her. "She still does." I placed a pair of socks on the stack. "She'd want you to be happy, you know? To remember the times you had together, but to put them away in your heart and get on with your life. She'll always be with you because she is you. You're her, too. One soul in two bodies, now only in yours."

I realized she'd stopped working. Felt her eyes upon me. When I looked up, there was that Grace Owen grin, sly as a fox.

She winked.

And I remembered.

I fell into her arms. This time she stayed until I let her go.

When I awoke, I was smiling.

≈ ≈

But I was still in the cavern. Unable to face the abyss. As badly as I wanted freedom, I simply couldn't bring myself to do it.

I'd grown content there. I was trapped, but at least I was safe. The third encounter changed all that.

≈ ≈

"Mom!" This time I knew where we were and what she was. I stood in the doorway to her room. Her back was to me. She was focused on packing a suitcase laying open on the bed. I approached and tried for a hug. She returned it half-heartedly, one-

armed, as if she'd had enough of the sappy stuff. Her focus remained on her work.

"Don't you love me?" I was only teasing—but still wanted to hear it.

"Read the drawin' wall." She squinted at two pairs of socks. She dropped one into the suitcase and tossed the other.

"Mo-ommm!"

"Read the drawing wall, Jesser-oodi. You'll see." She turned to me. "Any more questions before I go?"

As a matter of fact, I did have questions. Strangely, rather than sadness or loss, a sense of opportunity surged through me. After all, I was speaking with a ghost. "Okay, would you happen to know where I am, exactly?"

"Yep. You're in the quittin' place."

"What? That doesn't make any sense."

"Y' gave up, tough girl. You decided to quit."

I had never walked away from a fight in my life! I was the toughest in Taekwondo and had just clawed my way through an all-night ordeal with a human monster-truck. I deserved a little more credit than she was giving me. "Did not. I fought as hard as I could!"

"Yep, you sure did. For a while. Nice shot with the tire iron, by the way."

"And I kicked out the taillight."

"That, my little friend, was completely over the top."

She gestured for a high-five and I gave it.

"Okay so when, exactly, did I give up?"

The playful tone vanished. She stopped packing and turned to face me, hands on her knees. Squinting into my eyes, she asked, "Are you ready for this?" More to herself than me.

"Ready for what?"

She stared a beat longer, then nodded. "You quit when Master Pastor died. After everything else you'd been through, it was just more than you could handle." Her eyes pierced my soul. "So you quit."

━ ━

"He's real," he said. "I've seen Him." His face was greasy with sweat; his lips were blue. Bloody brown sludge oozed out between his fingers.

"Who's real?" I shook my head. "Never mind. Just try to relax."

He smiled— "No one can replace anyone else, right?" —and managed a pained chuckle. "But there is a position coming open."

"Don't talk like that."

"An important one."

"Please, Master Pastor!"

"I know the perfect one to fill it. But don't try too hard, Jess. Just . . . open your heart." He nodded— "Trust me." —then winked. "He'll find you."

I glanced up at the crackle of a radio. Twigs snapped, leaves rustled. An orange reflective vest came into view.

I leaped up. "Hey! Over here!" I waved my arms like crazy.

"I got her!"

Another voice called out in answer, then a third.

"They're here!" I looked down at Master Pastor. "You're going to be . . . "

His eyes were closed; his hands were clasped. Utterly unmoving.

At peace.

He was all I had left.

So I drifted away.

Just as far as my mind could take me.

━ ━

The third visitation continued:

"I prayed for him, Mom." I shook my head. "So did Mrs. James. And everyone else. Why didn't God answer our prayers?"

"God always answers prayers, little girl. Sometimes the answer is No."

I slowly nodded. "Well, Master Pastor never gave up. And neither did I."

"You're quittin' as we speak, pumpkin. Master Pastor taught you, 'Never give up'. But I got news for ya. The match that started in that parking lot ain't over yet."

"I made it to safety, didn't I?"

"You're safe from Machine Man. But you're not safe from what he did to you. He changed you, Jess.

Made you your own enemy. You're no longer safe from yourself."

— —

It hit me like a punch in the face.

The cavern was in my head!

This revelation made escape no easier. In fact, it seemed to seal me in. How could I escape from myself?

At the end of the third dream-visit, she told me.

— —

"So what can I do?"

"Finish the fight." She nodded, sure of herself. *"But, tough girl, the last round is with the thing in the abyss."*

I shuddered at the thought. "You'll help me, right?"

"Nope. This one's on you, Jessi. I've already done all I'm allowed to do here. But Mrs. James is tryin' to help."

Of course! The voice was Vivian James! I knew it was real! I knew I knew her!

"She's a good person, babe. And she's hurtin', too. You need her, but she needs you as well. Listen to her. Trust her, Jessi."

She looked me over one last time, then nodded. "Anything else, Jesser-oodi?"

"Well, yeah." I thought about it. What an opportunity here! I wanted to make the most of it.

So I asked the question to which everyone wants an answer: "Mom, is there really a God? I mean, have you met Him?"

She burst into guffaws. She bent and slapped her knee, stood and hugged her belly.

Her laughter faded, punctuated with chuckles and sighs. "Jessi, honey, if that's the best you can do . . . " She shook her head and took a breath. "Well, I got places to go, thangs to do, and people to see."

She tweaked my nose and just like that, we were out in the street. Mom was already two doors down, dancing a jig, slinging her suitcase. Snapping her fingers.

She yelled over her shoulder without looking back— "Don't forget to check the drawin' wall!" — then danced her way out of my life.

Epilogue

"You sure look pretty." Vivian James spooned a bite of oatmeal, scraped the excess on the rim of the bowl. According to the so-called "experts," Jessi processed little of what she saw and less of what she heard. *PTSD-Induced Catatonic Depression,* they said.

Hogwash. Textbook mumbo jumbo. They didn't spend every day with the child, cared nothing about her. They had no heart, no *feel* for her. Jessi was *right there,* taking in everything around her, at the very least on a subconscious level.

She dipped another bite— "Ready to talk to me today?" —and held it out to Jessi. "Or at least look at me?"

So she kept carefully concealed her embers of anger. It was not easy. Though a night's sleep had smothered the flames, memories of the conversation threatened to fan the embers, set them once more alight.

"That kid ain't your responsibility, you know."
Vivian scoffed. "Well if not mine, then whose?"
"Oh they got places. Special doctors and stuff."
"Special doctors." She spit out the words, barely avoiding actually spitting.

"I'm just sayin'. Spendin' ever' second cooped up with her—"

Vivian beetled her brow.

"—not to mention your last dime—"

"I've got plenty of—"

"—all for nothing. It don't seem healthy, you know? It just ain't right."

"Well, it's right for me."

The woman shook her head. "I'm tellin' you, Vivian. She's a ball and chain. You just settin' yourself up for a bad fall."

She found herself shaking. She jabbed her finger in the woman's face. "You better watch your mouth before you set yourself up for a bad fall!"

Vivian froze. Absently set the spoon in the bowl. "Jessi?" She'd seen something; she was sure of it. "Jessi."

Had Jessi's eyes moved? Indeed something seemed different today. Nothing specific, just . . . different. She cursed herself inwardly for letting her anger dull her edge.

She leaned in, squinting. "Jessi?"

= =

I awake, still trapped within the prison of my mind.

I sit up. Stand up. Find myself at the edge of the abyss.

Across the great divide, Vivian speaks to me: "Ready to talk to me today? Or at least look at me?"

I can see her there, through my real eyes—yet I'm unable to return her gaze. Nor can I control my lips to speak. "Mrs. James!" Only echoes in the cavern. I shout again, louder.

Silence.

I lean into a step.

I scramble back, nearly slip, teetering for balance. Rocks and soil crumble into the abyss, a granite on granite clacking that fades but never ceases.

Across the great divide, Vivian.

Within the abyss, hell.

My stomach churns. My heart pumps battery acid.

I close my eyes. Suck a breath.

I take the leap.

Falling, plummeting, I race through the years of my life ... my birth ... my first steps ... Blurry blissful baby babbling ... Mom and Dad, laughing ... Master Pastor, shouting. (I yell because I care!)

Scenery passing in a blur. School. Church. Sunshine and rain.

Two shots like thunder ... cold craters swimming with warm memories ...

Kind crystal blue eyes, someone's mother, bloody dripping hand ...

Naked to the world and the Devil himself, frightened and alone . . . Pain . . . So much blood . . .

A nice boy. Cute, too. Dumbo ears.
Brains tangled in my hair . . .

Master Pastor, my surrogate father, my best friend . . . Stepping down, bowing out, the champion defeated in his final bout.
Victorious.

I walk the gauntlet, teeth clenched, eyes wide open. Defiant.
"Hit me with all you've got!" I am done. Determined. Damned if I'll fail. (He'll have to kill me first.) I scream, but my lips don't move.

A silhouette. A great shadow blocking out the sun. Creeping toward me.
I shudder. Grit my teeth. I step forward, then again—closer now.
Chuckle as if from a demented giant. Something striking a concrete floor. Wooden. Rigid. Solid. Deadly.

I scream in terror, but I don't back down. I look him in the eyes.

He steps from the shadows, and my jaw drops.
He's just a boy. No older than me.

Hanging limp from his hand, a stick of wood like an old ax handle. His face is expressionless. Dead. He stands and stares.

Lost.

He spirals into a whirlwind of screams.

———

I am nowhere; now here. Looking out my own eyes.

Vivian speaks to me so sweetly.

She talks about Master Pastor: " . . . taught you not only how to survive, but how to *live*." She's holding a bowl in one hand, a spoon in the other at her lap. "I want you to *live*, baby. Not spend all day cramped up in this little room. I want to see you out in the *world*. Soaking up sunshine. Skipping through a field of daisies." She thought a minute, then added, *"Shopping!"*

———

I am so close; she's right in front of me. The breeze from the ceiling fan caresses my face. My real face.

"Mrs. James?"

But my lips won't move.

(Never give up).

"Mrs. James, I do *want* to live!" *Stronger now, still silent. Agonizing.*

⸺ ⸺

Vivian rose from the chair, turned and collected the dishes. Humming softly.

⸺ ⸺

"No! Wait! Don't go!" My lips are moving. My real lips. Just barely, but moving.

"Mrs. James! I want to live!" More this time . . . Oh please, God, keep her here. Don't let her walk away.

"Mrs. James!" Closer . . . Just a little more . . .

(He'll have to kill me first.)

I gather my breath, hands fisted at my sides, infuriated, determined.

"I! Want! To! LIVE!"

⸺ ⸺

"I want to live."

Vivian turned on her heel. The dishes crashed to the floor. The voice had been but a hoarse whisper, but unmistakable.

"*Jessi?*" She found herself kneeling at the chair, the girl's face in her hands. Her gaze went unreturned. But as she watched, a single tear escaped Jessi's eye and rolled down her cheek.

Vivian hugged her and wept, held her like she'd never let her go.

I want to live.

= =

Vivian never left my side. She'd moved into our house, the logic being that I'd be most comfortable there. She was careful to leave things exactly as she'd found them. So the house would still feel like my home.

Especially the drawing wall.

When I made it to my feet, Vivian walked me to the note Mom had left for me that September day seemingly eons ago.

Chalk flowers and rainbows. A girl in a Karate gi:

Welcome to the 5th grade, Jessi Owen!
Good luck at school today.
I love you so much,
Mom.

Perhaps she really had told me of the note in the dream-visit. Or perhaps I'd registered it as I passed—at least on a subconscious level—and inserted it into my dreams.

Or perhaps both.

What does it matter?

She never visited me again, not like in the visions. I dreamed of her from time to time—less often as the years passed—and even sometimes spoke with her there in the land of fantasy.

I still do.

But she's no longer real. Her replies are plastic. Phony.

She says what I expect her to say.

Vivian and I passed the years together, a mini misfit family. Dreadful as that day had been, it was *just* a day, and so it passed like every other day, as did all the sorrow and pain, as will every human being and every blade of grass, as is the way of things.

And they live on inside us, Dad and Mom, Master Pastor.

They live through us, teach through us. Through me. With the strength of their spirits, we fight the good fight until we're defeated in our final bout, like the warriors before us and like those yet to come, all of us survivors.

I sincerely hope you enjoyed *Finding Nowhere.* Your heart-felt review on Amazon will help guide readers who follow you.

And now here's an excerpt from *Drawer #7,* a psychological thriller with more twists than a hangman's noose.

DRAWER #7

-Born on Stage-

Blankets of smoke hung like fog in a cemetery; the mirror was clouded with layers of nicotine. But this much was certain: *That was not her face!*

Not her eyes staring back at her but then, what did her eyes look like anyway? She cocked her head, anticipating amusement when she realized what was happening.

No revelation enlightened her.

She inched forward for a closer look. No, definitely not her face.

Assess: I'd been . . .

Been doing what, exactly? And where?

Her memory was as blank as the eyes in the glass.

Well, what do *I remember?*
No farther back than maybe sixty seconds ago.

Spinning. She found herself spinning, woke up spinning, was seemingly *born* spinning, centripetal force flinging her hair wildly. Scenery passing in a blur. Her skull rattled with rhythmic pulses over which Rod Stewart husked something about being sexy and wanting his body. Her circling created a recurring Doppler effect, the pitch of the music rising and falling, rising and falling.

Motion sickness. A lump balled in her belly, exacerbated by the smell of . . . What was that *smell?*

Spinning.

She realized the pivot point was a thick brass pole, to which she was tethered by her own grip. Disoriented, she lost purchase on the metal—and tumbled to the floor like a discarded ventriloquist dummy. She sucked a hiss through her teeth and flipped her hair out of her face.

Spinning, now only in her head, eyes swimming, she propped herself on one elbow. Pin spots cut through a fetid haze like searchlights seeking an escaped convict. She squinted, shading her eyes from the slashing colored beams. Her nostrils stung with the overwhelming tang of cigarette smoke.

Still spinning, slower now, her eyes began to lock on images. Above her, suspended speakers. A distorted voice, torn to rags by the pounding beat, competed with the music. Beside her, the brass pole from which she'd just fallen. Beyond that, jeering faces shouted. Some waved . . . dollar bills? Why just faces and arms? Were they standing in a pit?

No. She herself was elevated somehow.

A stage?

A stage. With a brass pole. Before an audience.

She struggled to her feet and shaded her eyes from the blinding lights. Beyond the line of bellowing masks, a throng of silhouettes gestured wildly. *That* was the smell.

She grimaced at the pungency of oversexed bodies in unwashed clothes, all ripe with alcohol sweat—all men. Most were yelling, or maybe cheering, hands cupped to their mouths. Some whistled through circled fingers. A few doubled over with laughter.

The distorted voice vying for attention again: "Let's give it up for Star!"

She turned, tottered, nearly tripped. Emergency exit. Backdoor. Doggy door. *Anything.*

Instead, floor-to-ceiling mirrors presented other, more urgent concerns.

As expected, the glass revealed the usual mirror world, where right was left and front was back. There was the reversed stage on which she stood; backwards patrons jeered from deeper beyond the surface.

But what she saw within *this* fantasy world suggested other, more troubling opposites. Perhaps good was evil there. Perhaps people grew to infancy as they aged, for they were born dead.

It was the image of herself that disturbed her, that conjured the darkness. She saw her reflection, yes— but seeing in no way meant believing.

She was topless. A black leather g-string barely covered her in a studded triangle. The elastic straps holding it in place disappeared around her hips. She felt them now, meeting just below the dimples at the small of her back, turning south, disappearing into her gluteal cleft. Her ass, then, would be exposed to the fetid air of the club.

For the scrutiny of all.

Her feet were wedged into open-toed, chic black corset heels. Their leather straps wound almost to her knees. She struggled to maintain balance, teetering as she wriggled her toes.

(I said, let's give it up for Star! Hey! Star!)

The face.

This had to be a ruse of some sort. A wall-mounted screen? Some digital version of a funhouse mirror? Except even the peripherally visible shapes of her nose and lips were all wrong.

Like with anyone, the outermost aspects of her face were apparent. Accustomed to them, they remained beyond conscious notice. In the case of blemishes, makeup, or sometimes with certain wounds, the changed topography is quite apparent until we acclimate ourselves to it.

She could undoubtedly discern facial alterations in her peripheral, but no blemishes or irregularities of any kind marred the countenance in the glass. Injury free, the face was healthy and normal enough, except for the purple dyed tips of its brown hair. Just that, it wasn't *her* hair. Not her nose, not her lips, not her *face*.

Flummoxed, confused, she gently ran the fingers of her right hand over her eyes, nose, lips, throat . . .

(Star!)

A glance down at her real body proved the mirror 100% accurate in its assessment—if not brutal in its indifferent presentation.

She shifted her eyes back to the glass. In fact, she realized, that was not her body, either Not her breasts, not her legs, not even her toes peeking from the ends of the heels. As her focus shifted to the fingers tracing her body, the mirror revealed chipped red polish on bitten nails as if they belonged to a twelve-year-old.

Those were not even her hands!

Pursing her lips, wriggling her eyebrows, blinking—the face mimicked her every expression.

"JULES!"

She was snapped out of her reverie not by the DJ but by the more insistent acoustic voice booming for attention from behind her—and by the enormous body of the voice bumbling up onto the stage.

"What's wrong, baby girl?"

Assess: Black male. Maybe six-six, 300 pounds.

Instinctively, she crossed her arms to cover herself, right over left. Just as his right hand fell on her left shoulder, she seized the first three fingers of it in her right hand.

Adrenaline flooded her bloodstream. She ducked under his arm, twisting it as she skittered into place. Changing hands as she wound up behind him, she hyper-extended his fingers in her left fist, shooting his elbow skyward.

The refrigerator grimaced and teetered. She yanked down and body-checked him, *hard*.

Wind-milling his arms for balance, his size working against him, he careened into the brass pole, vibrating the entire stage. He slipped off the platform and onto a front-row table. Glass shattered and patrons scattered like cockroaches.

She confirmed his neutralization only peripherally, for her focus was on escape—getting *out,* waking *up,* getting *gone,* flying *free.*

Leaping from the stage, stumbling on the heels, dizzied by the dancing colored pin spots, dodging a drunk, colliding with a topless waitress balancing a tray of drinks *(Goddamn it, Star!),* she jostled her way toward the glowing exit sign, hands protecting her breasts.

Her left ankle turned painfully on the heels. She managed to catch herself on a baby-faced frat brother. His t-shirt exclaimed, *No means Yes and Yes means TRAIN!*

The punk took advantage of the moment for a quick grope. So she broke the left spike-heel off on his foot, chambering her knee nearly all the way to her collarbone. Her ankle screamed with the impact.

The boy crumbled to the floor. The pounding music swallowed his shouts of pain. She stomped the other heel off on the floor and shot into the crowd.

A man's suit jacket draped over the back of a chair. Grab it. Twirl it over her shoulders. That's it, faster now, picking up momentum, toward the exit, toward sanity.

Pushing and shoving her way through the crowd, she puzzled over her combat instincts. How had she done those things? Of what else was she capable?

She was dreaming. Had to be.

She slammed that square peg against the round hole of what her five senses were telling her, but it refused to penetrate.

A dead-eyed waitress stepped aside, barricading drunks with one hand, raising her tray above the path with the other.

But if not a dream, what was it? Who was *she?* Where had she come from?

Stop it!

Focus. Get the hell out of here.

Dodging another drunk, stepping over a spill, she worked her way through the maze of bodies and then—

"Where you think you going, *Cat?*" Another bouncer, a black Arnold Schwarzenegger, blocked the doorway with his bulk. *BT's,* apparently the name of this hellhole, was embroidered over his left pec. His massive chest stretched the letters like Play-Doh. Hands on his hips, he was a mountain, immovable. She glanced left, then right—then snapped her head left again.

Another mirrored wall. Panicked expression, slender arms, ivory skin stretched taut over thin legs, again she gawked at herself.

That's not me, damn it!

Why the amnesia? Was she in shock? Maybe on drugs? She felt sober. Lucid. She'd never taken an illegal substance in her life. *(And how do I know this?)* But perhaps she'd been slipped something?

By whom? And for what purpose?

Perhaps she'd suffered a head injury. She felt no pain or dizziness, save for the effects of the dancing lights and second-hand smoke, which was no doubt laced with weed.

Or maybe this was a nightmare after all, and she'd soon wake up.

But wake up *where?* If it wasn't a dream, where was she *now? Who* was she?

Reality intruded when the bouncer's fist clamped around her left upper arm. She spied another topless waitress with a tray of drinks. Just within reach.

In one quick motion, she seized the neck of a frosty Corona, hand flipped thumb-side down, and arced it over her shoulder. The container shattered over the bouncer's head.

Blinded by suds and shards of glass, he released her, more concerned now with swiping slivers from his face without further lacerating himself.

She slipped past and slammed into the push-bar of the front door.

She stumbled to a stop. The door eased shut behind her, muting the chaos and Rod Stewart's husky crooning. Incongruously, a cool breeze lightly caressed her hair. Halogen lights provided a glowing blanket for the cars dozing in the lot. She took a deep breath. Released it slowly. The fresh air calmed her, but she knew better than to relax.

Silence, save for the sound of her breathing.

Hugging the jacket tightly around her, she desperately surveyed the lot. Heart pounding. She felt like a damn Dutch milkmaid in the broken-heel footwear, toes turned skyward ridiculously. She was ready to bolt, *yearning* to run.

But to *where?* Her mind offered no memories of a home—no car, no pet, no friends, no past.

She stood frozen, shackled by indecision. Behind her the strip joint. To her left a six-foot wooden fence. Straight ahead a dumpster. Hide behind it? Burrow into the garbage? No, they'd find her.

Somewhere in the distance, a dog barked.

To her right, a four-lane roadway divided by a median. The susurration of light traffic was somehow comforting, but she fought its lulling effects.

Hotwire a car?

Now how did she know she could do that? Or *could* she do it? Maybe the ability to steal a car was part of her nightmare. No, she knew she could do it, in too much detail to be a dream. Still, she couldn't do it fast enough to avoid apprehension. Countless questions bombarded her, threatening to bury her in unwanted distractions.

The door burst open, behind it surely the beer-soaked bouncer, thoroughly pissed. Shouts from deeper inside the club edging closer *(Little shit stole my jacket!),* Rod Stewart now un-muted, blasting something about letting him know—smoke roiled out, engulfing her in a malignant cloud.

Without risking even a moment to glance back, she bolted for the highway, jacket billowing, just as fast as her Dutch milkmaid clogs would carry her.

-Yacht-

There was no rhyme or reason for it—no correlation to sleep, caffeine or anything else he could figure. It just came and went as it pleased, and to hell with whateve he happened to be doing at the time.

Sometimes it felt as if the storm had finally passed, almost as if it had never happened at all—not really. And even if it had, the memories were nothing more than the stuff of dreams long forgotten. He fell for it every time, allowed himself to believe only better days lay ahead, that he was finally through it.

Those were the good days.

Other days were not so good. On bad days—days like today—the memories roiled like storm clouds, the promise of the nightmare pelting him like sheets of frozen rain.

On "hail days," he focused on his work.

The Tiger Saw was a bronco, crazy with panic, plaster shrapnel flying like foam from its bladed mouth. The tool bucked and gyrated, desperate to throw its rider and gallop free. Freddie "the Fixer" Schaeffer clung stubbornly to the molded plastic. Teeth clenched, forearms bulging. Refusing to relinquish his mount.

He knelt in a sweltering attic, bent to his task. The glow from a dangling forty-watt bulb cut through abandoned cobwebs and cast agitated shadows in the growing cloud of dust. Through drywall and rafters alike, he inched along the two- by three-foot rectangle he'd drawn, careful to maintain his tenuous balance and death grip on the saw. The noise was horrendous.

After what seemed an eternity, the section of ceiling finally gave way. It crashed to the kitchen floor below, sucking much of the dust along with it. Freddie rose with a grimace and balanced on parallel rafters. After a moment, he removed his safety goggles. At six-four, it was necessary to contort himself to stretch his back. He stood staring down through the dust.

(Subsonic vibrations)

What was the next step? Framing? Fine adjustments to the opening?

(Creeping through his feet, into his legs)

Prep the shelving unit? Set up the saw horses? Take a break? Come on, think!

(Rumbling, so low it registered only in his spine)

Frame. Springs. Tools. Fasteners. What was the next step?

(Lift the beam somehow. Quick! What could serve as a lever? A fulcrum? Come on, think!)

His legs trembled and his hands shook. The square hole he'd just cut morphed into a jagged maw, the drywall massive plates of ravaged concrete. Stray slivers of rafter were mangled fingers of rebar. The eight-foot drop to the kitchen floor yawned to a bottomless chasm, at the bottom of which lay—

"What the hell are you doing to my *house?*" Joe Zaydon laughed, peering up from below. Joe was the owner of the house. He waived away dust and repositioned himself to locate Freddie in the gloom.

"You think this is a shock, wait 'til you see my final bill."

The banter dissipated the daydream, rumble receding like dying thunder. Freddie lowered the Tiger Saw by the cord.

By unspoken agreement, Joe retrieved the tool and eased it to the kitchen floor. "We're headed out. If we're not back before you're done for the day, just lock up behind yourself."

Hands on his knees, Freddie leaned over the hole and smiled. "Say, where do you keep the valuables?"

Joe chuckled as he walked away. "Under a tarp in the yacht out back," he called over his shoulder.

The front door opened . . . closed . . . then all was silent.

Only Joe Zaydon could coax a chuckle from Freddie on a hail day. There was no yacht. Probably nothing more than a swim noodle back there. The Zaydons had five daughters, all home-schooled by their mother Dymphna. Joe owned a flower shop downtown and did okay. Still, with one income and seven mouths to feed, they struggled. Freddie was doing the job at cost.

No other handyman would have even attempted the project regardless of the price. Freddie was a solid craftsman, no genius but smarter than most. While he could tackle any run-of-the-mill repairs and construction, his specialty lay in solving unorthodox problems. Building a loft with no ground support. Erecting a tree house. Creating a waterproof hole in the ground for the drop-pin of a chain link fence gate.

He'd once installed a backyard firing range for a cop in Pinecrest. The code department had told him, *You show us blueprints for a structure that will A, be soundproof, and B, contain stray rounds fired in any direction, we'll approve the permit.* In other words, no.

The next day, Freddie had shown up with plans for an underground range, complete with sump-pump drainage and ventilation system. The city had reluctantly granted the permit.

His uncanny ability to resolve seemingly impossible problems was not only a source of income but an effective distraction from thoughts of the past. Usually.

Today, he was adding storage space to an already crowded kitchen. Most times, conventional wisdom generated the answer, *It can't be done.* So Freddie avoided conventional wisdom, gently easing it from his thoughts as he assessed the issue. His clever solutions always began with an objective assessment of the problem, then proceeded with a completely open mind as to the solution. He allowed his imagination to roam free, much farther astray than most were comfortable.

With the storage space puzzle, when his mind had concluded there was utterly no space in the kitchen in which to start, he'd simply refused to accept it. Instead, he posed a question: *Where* is *space available?*

As he'd peered around the counters and cabinets with Joe, his gaze had wandered upward. "Do you have much headroom in the attic?"

"Sure. But I don't want to climb the folding ladder every time we need a frying pan!"

"You won't have to."

Construction of any kind works only as well as the parts from which it's created. Loathe to let his mind wander, Freddie climbed down from the attic and headed to his van for the stainless-steel shelving system he'd recommended.

The unit weighed ninety pounds. Printed on the side of the box, within a green circle, was a simple graphic of a man carting a box on a hand truck, crescent smile under dot eyes. Beside it, within a red slashed circle, the same figure strained to lift the box. Droplets of cartoon sweat squirted from his head, a lightning bolt at his lower back.

Freddie hefted the box and threw it over one shoulder. At six-four, 250 pounds, he could lift a bag of Quikrete, or a stainless-steel shelving unit, as if it were a sack of sugar. His size made him clumsy in enclosed spaces. But outside in his element, he thrived.

This genetic strength did not automatically come with a lean and cut physique. He was solidly built but by no means a bodybuilder. Nor was he a model. Though far from homely, his mug was that of a boxer—like a beating with an ax handle would leave his face no worse for the wear, the wielder of the weapon spent.

He cut his own hair, and only "when it needed it." When it got out of control, he'd buzz it down to a bur with dog shears, after which he'd dedicate about as much thought to the matter as a bear did to table manners. After a year or so, his mane would morph back into what it was now: a boyish, shoulder length, disheveled mop.

Style concerned him not in the least. He had no business meetings to attend. Nor was he plagued by thoughts of courting. He'd carefully constructed for himself a life of simplicity. His friends were more acquaintances, consisting for the most part of satisfied clients. He was content with his loneliness, or pretended to be.

He plugged in his saws and set up wooden horses on the patio. Over the next several hours, he framed out the hole, being sure to include firm support for the garage door springs. He ran cables and measured space for the counterweights. When he realized the sun was going down, he picked up the pace, careful to compensate for his growing fatigue. His desire to see the solution work was stronger than his need for rest.

Nearing completion, his excitement grew. He wrestled the stainless-steel shelving unit up the folding ladder to the attic. He attached the cables, springs and folding arms.

Back down in the kitchen, he stared up at the new door on the ceiling. He reached up, grasped the handle and pulled gently. With a yawning of springs not unlike those of the attic door, the unit coasted down.

Freddie smiled.

Life should be so simple.

He swept the kitchen and patio, wound his cords, collected his tools and blew his saws free of dust. He loaded it all into the van.

Freddie loved the old bucket, a 1992 Dodge Ram. Old but reliable, he'd named her "Mable." Old Mable. White paint long since dulled, it featured faded logos on the sides, hood, and rear cargo doors: *Freddie the Fixer.*

Back in the day, he'd picked her up at a Bellsouth auction. A steal of a deal, of course, meant it needed some work, but hey—that's what Freddie did. He'd replaced the seals, dropped in a new transmission and lubed her up good. After a shot of gloss white paint, she was ready to roll.

He was pleased with his cargo compartment design, a system of roll out shelves installed on gate rollers, the tracks welded to the interior bed. Heading for Old Mable at the end of the day was almost as sweet as heading for home.

The sun had long since retreated over the horizon. He locked up the house, chuckled at the non-existent yacht and hopped in the van. He keyed the ignition, and Old Mable rumbled to life. Switching on the headlights, he threw her in gear and swung out onto the open road.

Freedom at last. The day the earth yawned beneath him had not so much as crossed his mind. Nor had Stevie. What had started as a hail day had turned out sunny.

He was content with a good day's work and proud of a job well done.

~Hit n Run~

She'd been making it, damn it. Outta there, into the blue, history. Then the van.

Determined footsteps on her heels, assaulted by incensed shouts of anger, she'd cut through traffic in the northbound lanes.

Under threat, attack what's attacking you.

Where had she heard that?

Across the northbound lane, she'd vaulted the curb of the median. She'd bolted through the grass, arms tucked tightly to her sides, over the left curb of the southbound traffic—then *WHAM!*

Two more inches and she'd have made it. It was the damn heels. Or what was left of them.

Tires screeching, the jalopy had struck her right buttock. She'd gone sailing through the air spinning clockwise but managed to somehow "cat-twist" as she flew. She'd relaxed into it—then tucked her head and rolled when she landed. *What was that?*

Now she stood facing the van, owl-eyed driver gawking through the windshield. Glaring angry mob to her right across the highway. They shouted and gestured rabidly, waiting for traffic to clear.

She looked at the driver. He was taking in the scene across the highway.

She jerked her head right to the mini-mob.

Then straight ahead to the driver (he now returned her glance).

Then back to the mob.

The bouncer and leader of the gang took the first steps of a head start across the road, emphatically waving a car past. *(Hurry up, fool!)* With an angry honk, the car swerved to miss him—and the way was clear.

She cut her eyes back to the van. The driver leaned quickly over and unlocked the passenger door.

Keep running or hop in the van? She didn't know the driver but could safely assume he was "Freddie the Fixer," since it was emblazoned mirror image across the front of the hood.

The mob was almost upon her.

She bolted for the passenger door, yanked it open and vaulted inside.

"Go. *GO!*" she yelled, just as the bouncer flashed across the headlight beams and scrambled around to her side.

"Go!"

Tires peeling rubber, they surged forward.

She tried to shut the door. Something obstructed it. The bouncer, lacerated face grimaced in rage. His left hand gripped the doorpost, his right the door itself. Hanging on stubbornly. The smell of Corona and cologne-sweat flooded the cab as he strained to keep up.

She hopped onto her left knee. Braced her right hand on the dash. She stomped her broken right heel into his face. Once, twice, then the third kick hit nothing but air when the bouncer finally let go. He stumbled to the pavement. Shouts indiscernible as he faded, kneeling on the road behind them, he swung his fists wildly in the air.

She slammed the door shut.

End Excerpt.

Books by Jeff Wade

Dread
Finding Nowhere
Drawer #7

Correspondence:

Jeff Wade
JeffWade.com
Jeff@JeffWade.com
786-290-4603